To Gary from

Malcolm McPherson

4·18·97

MATRIARCHY
Freedom in Bondage

Matriarchy: Freedom in Bondage
An Illuminated Novel by Malcolm McKesson
HECK Editions, First Edition January 1997

All text and art copyright ©1997 by Malcolm McKesson.
Introduction © 1996 Tony Thorne
Edited by Wesley Gibson and K. Gates. Designed by K. Gates and Davi Det Hompson

ISBN: 0-9638129-7-1 (softcover)   0-9638129-8-X (hardcover)
Library of Congress Cataloguing in Publication Card Number: 96-077595

HECK Editions is an imprint of Gates of Heck, Inc.
954 Lexington Avenue, Suite 118, New York City, NY   10021
http://www.heck.com   (212) 879-5016

Available thorugh D.A.P./Distributed Art Publishers
636 Broadway, 12th Floor, New York, NY   10012
Tel: (212) 473-5119   Fax: (212) 673-2887

Printed in Hong Kong

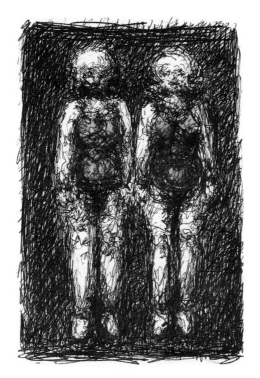

Boy and Girl Dressed Alike

Malcolm McKesson is represented by

Henry Boxer Gallery
98 Stuart Court
Richmond Hill, Richmond
Surrey, England TW10 6RJ
ph: 1 (81) 948 1633

Malcolm McKesson as a young man

MATRIARCHY
Freedom in Bondage

Malcolm McKesson

Introduction by Tony Thorne
Edited by Wesley Gibson and Katharine Gates

New York
HECK Editions
1997

And His Little Mistress.

CONTENTS

The Reclusive World of Malcolm McKesson

by Tony Thorne

A lifetime of secretive creation led the newly revealed Malcolm McKesson to create an intensely personal world of dark, emerging figures, each playing an eerie role in complex courtship rituals and obsessive ceremony.

"To reroute, develop and elaborate – albeit with an adult's capacity for concentration and perseverance impulses... springing directly from early childhood." Thus, Michel Thévoz's definition of the practice of the Outsider Artist. Later in the same essay Thévoz claims that the Outsider Artist "must grapple with the child within... rather than with Raphael, Rembrandt or Picasso." The New York artist Malcolm McKesson, in a body of work only recently revealed, seems to unite the intensity of obsessional personal vision with a style which is Rembrandt-like in its assurance and texture and which recalls Balthus and Bellmer in its dark eroticism.

McKesson, now 87 years old, lives alone in a set of rooms in an otherwise elegant Manhattan hotel where for years past he has been working in ecstatic seclusion to produce a series of finely wrought drawings of a timeless fantasy world; a world with its own secret narratives, ceremonies and rules. His voluptuous, anonymous, androgynous figures seem to emerge from a soft muffling darkness, taking on form like a photographic plate slowly yielding an image. These mysterious, indistinct, courtly marionettes pose, merge, bow and submit in a dream landscape where unknown rituals are enacted in a state of erotic trance. McKesson himself gives the onlooker the keys to this vision in the form of captions inscribed in his fine, classical calligraphy on the reverse of the drawings. "I slowly danced my little intimate love dance to win his heart," is one such, "Even lovers must part at a clap and pay deep reverence," reads another. The secret of McKesson's art is a remarkable inner mythology, nurtured and elaborated over a span of sixty-odd years. He has judged that the time is now right to share his images with an audience who, following an overwhelming response at Outsider Art Shows in New York, he thinks will be receptive to this particular series of drawings (he had previously exhibited only concentrated studies of galleons, architectural arches, details of furniture) and the subversive messages and ideas that they carry within them.

In person the artist is far from the stereotype of the inarticulate, driven outsider. With the gravitas and charm and occasional vagueness of advanced age, he is eager, even anxious, to explain the search for maturity and for liberation which is symbolized in the juxtapositions of his shadowy, fleshy beings of indeterminate age and sex. He is telling, he says, a story which is medieval and modern at the same time, and which harks back, too, to an Atlantean age before man and woman were separable and in conflict. The characters in this stately pageant: pages, courtiers, choruses, forbidden lovers, act out subservience, dominance and confinement, chastising and chiding, blessing and forgiving. They are muzzled, bound and corseted, disguising and effacing personal identities and the outward signs of sexuality; male finery becomes indistinguishable from femininity (McKesson strongly disapproves of the puritan masculine fashions of this century) and woman as mother, *grande dame*, or mistress receives homage from the willingly humbled man. McKesson imagines the hermetic chiaroscuro setting of this lingering dream as an exclusive, hidden society, an academy or perhaps a court. As he describes it, it becomes clear that he is exploring familiar, even obvious, sexual and psychological archetypes, but through an expression which is entirely without sensationalism, worldliness or crass overstatement.

When he talks of his outer "real" life McKesson is matter-of-fact, but somehow his observations on his early years – a fairly privileged education, hints of parental disapproval, a period as a businessman in the Twenties and Thirties, religious disillusion, service in the US army overseas, are fleeting and rather uninvolved: he cites dates with an air of uncertainty and there are real or feigned memory lapses. Only isolated incidents – the early death of a sister, the discovery in Bavaria of "ugly and ferocious" illustrations from Nazi literature – seem real and engaging to him now. In was in 1961, with the support of his wife, the poet Madeline Mason, that Malcolm McKesson withdrew from the world of commercial, family and social commitments to dedicate himself to art and to a marriage which he says "revealed the strength and wisdom of the female" and only ended after 48 years with Mason's death in 1990. In his private meditations he set himself to confronting the inner dilemma, in his words, of "an adult, ill-equipped to establish a link with the spiritual."

Talking of the working processes McKesson says, "When I draw, I attempt to see the form of the undrawn... this is therapeutic for me." In terms of ideas, "I want to rediscover a buried tradition, to rediscover the female in the man; I've looked for a long time for a social dimension to all this; maybe now the world is ready for this sort of thing..."

The results of this process are the scores of drawings, each "labored over for an hour or so, in a state of intensely wonderful excitement," but McKesson has declared that the end-product of this life is to be a greater work; an epic illustrated autobiography, a fictionalized idealized and realized version of his lifetime struggle to define himself. The manuscript, entitled "Matriarchy", and consisting of more than twenty chapters, is heavily illustrated in pen and ink and is now virtually complete, in spite of the vertigo and nausea which has afflicted McKesson during its making, and despite his continuing doubts about the wisdom of self-revelation.

Tony Thorne

Without any thought of financial gain or celebrity and with a kind of innocence but none of the faux-naif about him, the reclusive McKesson is now coming into contact ("coming out" as he has put it) with more than one younger generation of appreciators, confessing that he is still surprised that his themes, with their overtones of bondage and transvestism as well as chivalry and courtly love, are today palatable to strangers.

Haunting, decorous, sinister but tender, the inhabitants of McKesson's pictures represents "a fantasy with a happy ending" and their world, according to their creator, is "powerfully sexual but always beautiful." The hero of both the drawings and the manuscript is, he says, "a confused young man who finds his strength in servitude." It is easy, if perhaps too glib, to see the parallels with the artist, old now, but still struggling with his dominant muse in the seclusion of his somber hotel suite. What astonishes is that this is not a momentary cathartic confrontation, but literally a lifetime of encounters; the real, urbane McKesson, in cap and muffler, diffidently moving about the New York interior, and his alter ego, the plump, powdered page straining to please his demanding mistress in the shadowy confines of the dream academy.

Tony Thorne is the author of "The Dictionary of Popular Culture" published by Bloomsbury, London. He broadcasts and lectures worldwide on issues of culture and language, and heads a department at King's College, University of London.

This article first appeared in __Raw Vision__ in 1994.

my Book
Matriarchy - Freedom In Bondage

This is a semi fantasy of a lost opportunity for true expression of servitude at early maturity.

I fall under the spell of a forceful woman who subjects me to her will with love and domesticates me in a feminine environment.

This do I show in advance of the time when I in fact marry, this fantastic mirage incarnated as my wife of 48 years.

Along the way, I break free from a dormant family relationship, my parents no longer capable of handling the weaning process; I also free my sister who blossoms in her own individuality.

The message is that children are born to a destiny not comprehended by their parents, however responsible they be.

True love of friends can repair the damage of the weaning process.

Malcolm McPherson

1.27.95

LETTER TO HENRY BOXER

My Book
Matriarchy- Freedom In Bondage

This is a semi-fantasy of a lost opportunity for true expression of servitude at early maturity.

I fall under the spell of a beautiful woman who subjects me to her will with love and domesticates me in a feminine environment.

Thus do I grow in advance of the time when I in fact marry, this fantastic mirage incarnated as my wife of 48 years.

Along the way, I break free from a dominant family relationship, my parents no longer capable of handling the weaning process; I also free my sister who blossoms in her own individuality.

The message is that children are born to a destiny not comprehended by their parents, however responsible they be.

True love of friends can repair the damage of the weaning process.

Malcolm McKesson

1.27.95

I thought you would like to have a little account of my obsession with love and slavery as a background to my art. So I give you this story illustrating the fantasy.

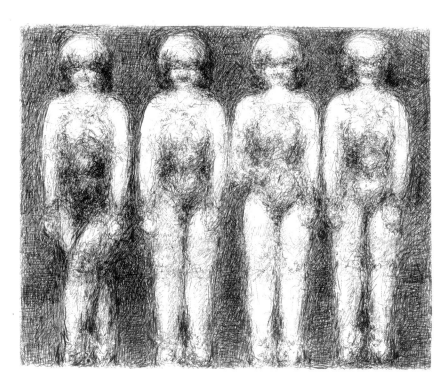

Presentation

Matriarchy

Freedom In Bondage

Malcolm McKesson

1·27·95

Book One:

ROSE

Sexless head

Book One | *Rose*

CONTENTS

PRISONER

I am a young man in all the beauty of youth. I have a keen desire to submit myself to a kind and beautiful woman of possessive will, who will allow me to be her slave.

I realize the danger of such a submission and so shun any such expression in all reality.

The year is 1929. My name is Gerald Graham. I am eighteen years old and about to enter Harvard, but immature in body and soul. I live with my parents and older sister in Manhattan. My mother is cruel and domineering, especially over my sister whose self-confidence she has slowly rooted out and destroyed. I myself have no sense of purpose and do not understand my own desires.

It is on a school ski trip that I meet my wonderful hostess, Miss Gladys von Gunthardt. As we sit in our compartment on the train, we speak of my dreams and youthful confusion. For the first time in my life someone has asked my opinion! When she later invites me to visit her for tea, I accept the invitation with joy.

I am received in a gorgeous mansion by a maid and conducted to a parlor where I am cordially greeted by my great hostess and invited to sit beside her on a couch between two shaded lamps. I am terribly impressed by the grandeur of this West Side mansion with marble front and iron fretworks and gate. The great parlor is hung with beautiful paintings in gold frames and the decor is opulent in the Edwardian manner. I feel out of my depth in this splendor and elegance.

We speak of many things and my hostess urges me to reveal my aspirations and philosophy. As we drink tea and eat delicious sand-

Prisoner

wiches, a wise old maidservant draws the curtains and lights the room. We also have a glass of rose wine.

After tea is removed, the lady draws me close to her and, in a motherly fashion, embraces me and comforts me, sympathizing with the dilemmas of my youth. Gradually I fall under the spell of her beautiful voice and touch, and find myself relaxing in her enveloping bosom as it rises and falls with her rhythmic breathing.

I awaken and am terrified to think that I have trespassed upon the hospitality of my lady by sleeping in her lap.

Overcome with remorse, I humbly beg her forgiveness. She tells me that she understands my predicament and urges me to stay.

"Don't be afraid, child," she says, "you may stay as long as you like. Sally will prepare dinner for us and we shall have a beautiful dinner together. But first let us change the relation between us and play that you are my dear child and I am your loving mother. Sally has a beautiful costume for you to wear and we shall play out our parts."

I am a little frightened but submit to the lady's sweet invitation, feeling a natural inclination to play.

The lady rings for the maid and instructs her to take me in hand and prepare me as her little son. She is to return me to her at 8 p.m. when we shall have dinner.

Sally bows and goes to the foyer, where she awaits me in compliance with the mistress' command.

She pats my cheek encouragingly and says: "Now go, child, and let Sally prepare you for our lovely evening together."

I rise obediently, drying my tears with my handkerchief and hasten to my fate.

Without a word, the maid proceeds up the carpeted stairs, indicating I should follow.

We enter a second-floor parlor. The maid instructs me to undress and opens the door to a bathroom where I am to bathe. She leaves the room, closing and locking the door The key sounds in the lock. I hang my jacket on the back of a chair, remove my shoes and socks, undo my necktie. Carefully, I drape my shirt and pants on the chair. I remove my underwear and enter the bathroom, where I take a delicious hot shower, anticipating with trembling the outcome of this great adventure.

I open the shower curtains and find before me the maid holding a great towel. Before I can utter my astonishment at being naked before a stranger, the woman proceeds to vigorously dry my trembling body.

She then removes a straight razor from the medicine cabinet and says: "I will now depilate your entire body. This will enhance your sensitivity to the textures of your clothing."

The blade of the razor is cool against my skin and I watch her with apprehension, hoping that she will not slip and cut me. But Sally is expert at her task, and before long I am as smooth and soft as an infant. She then applies cream to my body and face, which she also powders and perfumes.

Then without another word she seizes my hand in a grip of iron and leads me into the other room, where she dresses me in a silken bodice that starts at the crotch and straps over the shoulders. She corsets me in tightly from the back, handling my scrotum expertly so that my penis rises under the pressure of the silk. The strings at my back are tightened more and more as I draw in my breath and my waist contracts. She feels and smooths the silk and my body. I am sheathed from crotch to neck.

I am set into a chair and nylon hose are drawn over my legs and up to my waist, like panty-hose. My feet are put into high-heeled slippers which are fastened at the ankle.

My head is then adorned with a wig, the same color as my natural hair, and is fitted closely to my skull.

My arms, held forward, are slipped into lace sleeves that tie at the back. Tight kid gloves are worked over my fingers and buttoned at the wrist and a ring is fitted over each little finger.

A delicate chiffon veil is drawn over my face and secured at the nape of my neck.

My Nurse Sally then pulls a riding crop from a cabinet.

She speaks.

"Little one, you will now learn to walk gracefully in your slippers until the feel of them becomes natural. Walk with your weight on the heel. Do you understand?"

I murmur assent and stagger toward the great full-length mirror, my hand in the maid's grip. When I stumble I feel the sting of the horsewhip. My appearance in the mirror echoes my feeling of imprisonment. As a final touch, I am allowed to see the effect through the veil while a tight necklace of pearls is bound at the neck.

Thus attired, I am left alone to practice my steps. Carefully balancing on my heels and feeling the effects of my new bondage, I walk painfully about the room. I look for the chair where I had put my male clothing. All are gone! I look about the room and nearly fall as I realize that the clothes are no longer available to me. I am a prisoner in this house and the formidable maid, who now re-enters the room, is my keeper. She makes this very apparent by stinging my buttocks with the whip in her hand.

"Now, child, you will descend alone and present yourself to your mistress." Thus speaks my captor, opening the doorway which leads to the hall.

Correction

THE FIRST LESSON

bediently I teeter through the door under the watchful eye of my trainer, for such she has become. I am filled with the desire to do justice to my unfamiliar role and succeed in reaching the great baluster of the stairway. I grip it as a swimmer holds to the side of a pool when learning to swim.

Placing my feet carefully upon first step, I concentrate, place all my weight on the heels. The straps of the slippers are tight and prevent my foot from sliding forward into the shoe. I achieve the ground floor and sense the cold hard surface of the marble.

I rest and catch my breath. I must make a graceful entrance and stand before my mistress reverently, as the maid had done. Breathing is a little hard in my silken corset; I seek my composure. Then I advance resolutely, for I am awaited.

I come to the entrance, step forward and with my gloved hand turn the door knob. Opening the door, I furtively observe the familiar figure of my lady mistress reading at the lamp. I turn to close the door, with as much elegance as I can currently muster, turn again and stand before my Goddess. I take half a step back with my right leg, which I bend slightly. Bowing, I avert my gaze from her face to the floor.

I hold my position for some time, thinking my mistress had not observed my entrance.

Finally, I venture to peer up through my veil and see that my lady is observing me with a fixed gaze. My hands are at my side and I feel my thighs through the stockings. My knees are touching and I am balancing precariously.

The First Lesson

Page Boy

"Well, child, I can tell you that you are indeed beautiful. Sally is to be congratulated. I hope you behaved yourself under her skillful hands. Come now, let me see how you walk in your pretty slippers."

I carefully advance some three paces toward her and resume my reverence, not daring to look up.

"Poor child. I know you have so much to learn, as you surely will. For from this moment you shall be my 'Little Rose' and will learn all the graces ordinarily reserved for ladies. Come here, child, and kneel before me."

I move slowly to prevent falling and take a long step, bringing down my right knee and then my left, assuming the attitude of a supplicant, for I am indeed begging for forbearance with my awkwardness.

"Come forward to be kissed, darling."

I shuffle forward on my knees, sensing the rough nap of the carpet. In tears of fear and joy. I bury my head in my lady's hands, knowing this to be the moment of truth in my young life.

My lady takes my chin in her hand and kisses my lips through the veil.

"I shall explain to you the purpose of the veil, dear Rose. It is to smooth your once manly cheeks. In time, I shall teach you cosmetics and then you may indeed pass for my dear little daughter. Did you hear me, child? You are to be my little girl and study beauty in everything. When you have passed the test, you shall wear pretty dresses and serve me in public ways. But do not fear for your native sex, dear child - you shall be at times my little man child, at others my little girl. Yet you will always delight in the feminine, which will become your true nature. As a young man, you will forever be my dependent and rejoice in my service. As a young lady, you will rejoice in your beauty and guard your virginity."

Rose puts his palms together as a token of his understanding.

The First Lesson

"You are really very pretty, my dear, and I shall gild the lily by pinning this little rose corsage at your left breast."

This she does and kisses me again.

"Now, let us play a little until it is time for dinner. I want you to practice walking and then learn to fetch me things as I command.

"Get up now!"

I rise.

I essay to walk elegantly, when Madame orders me to stop.

"Rose dear, this will never do. I have a device which will guide you in your walking."

Madame rings for the maid.

"Sally, dear, we have a little time before dinner to train our boy to walk. I want you to get the Walking Machine."

"Yes, Madame," replies the maid and leaves the room with a curtsy.

I stand there, facing the wall, waiting and wondering. What is this Walking Machine and how will it train me to move gracefully in high heels?

Presently, I hear behind me the rolling of an object, perhaps a table, into the room.

"Rose! You will now submit to instructions from your nurse, Sally. Proceed, Sally, with the instruction."

"Yes, my lady," says Sally. "Turn around, little Rose, and give me your attention. This walking machine will give you balance. You must learn to walk gracefully in your pretty slippers. Do you understand? You may call me Miss Sally."

"Yes, Miss Sally. I am prepared for your instruction."

I look upon the device, beautifully worked in the finest wood. From the side it is shaped like an "H", about my height, with two horizontal bars. The lower bar is padded and at the height of my crotch and the upper, which has a kind of collar in the middle, is at the level of my chin. The two vertical bars rest on pairs of wheels, and attached to the front vertical at a convenient height is a set of handlebars.

"Very well, then," says Sally. "This rolling device is for you to stand in. See, I lower this bar padded in the middle. You will straddle the bar which I shall raise to a convenient height. Do so now."

I bend down under the two handlebars and raise one leg over the padded bar. The bar is then raised and secured so that my crotch presses down upon the padding. With my legs straightened, I rest my legs on the heels of my slippers. Nurse then secures the bar front and back so that I ride it like a stile. She adjusts my scrotum free of the stile. I maintain my balance by gripping the handlebars.

Now, the nurse secures the collar on the top horizontal bar around my neck and adjusts the height of the bar so that my head is stretched in place. My chin is thus held high, my posture erect and proud.

"Now, my child, you will walk and move about the room, guiding the machine with your hands. Do so now!"

Thus, fixed in position, I walk forward, passing before my mistress, turning and walking back. The machine rolls with greatest ease and steadies my body at the neck and at the crotch. If I miss my footing it is painfully disciplinary.

Thus, I was trained like a horse in the stocks for what seemed like a long time. I accommodated myself to the machine in order to avoid riding the bar and so learned how to walk in my new foot gear. With practice it would come to feel as if I were a part of the machine.

"Very well for now, Sally," spoke my mistress. "Remove Rose from the machine and take him to the dining room and teach him to serve. I shall be alone tonight. Commence dinner when it is ready."

"Yes, my lady," replied the maid.

The First Lesson

So I was disengaged from the machine, which was removed. I stood quietly while the nurse did this, and observed that my mistress had returned to her reading and dismissed me from her mind.

I thought to myself that my veil would prevent me from eating just as much as serving the dinner would.

I SERVE DINNER

ose found himself again in the firm grip of his nurse. She led him into the dining room and away from the supervision of his lady mistress. He was brought into the pantry and quickly outfitted with a black slip, black serving dress, lace apron and a cap for his hair.

Surveying the result, Sally shook her head with dissatisfaction. She removed the slip and dress and apron. From a closet she removed some padded silken forms. These were strapped tightly to his shoulders and waist, adding a more feminine shape to his thighs, breasts and buttocks. In this upholstery Rose was indeed a proper woman prepared to assume the black dress, the slip and the elegant apron of a serving maid.

Now Sally was pleased with me and declared that I would do.

Then she assumed a different attitude, one of professional instruction between familiars.

She instructed me to remove all chairs from the table, except that of my lady, and to set a proper table with napkins, a soup plate, knives, forks, spoons, and glasses. I curtseyed, holding my skirt, then turned and exited through the pantry. Smoothing my apron, I felt the full breadth of my midsection. My uniform was of purest silk and I was most happy.

I had concluded that my nurse hated the male sex, regarding the entire gender as unmanageable and awkward. Therefore, I determined that in her presence I would be as girlish as I could. When dressed in male attire, I would assume a particular reverence and childlike love. I knew that my masculinity was simply a masquerade.

I Serve Dinner

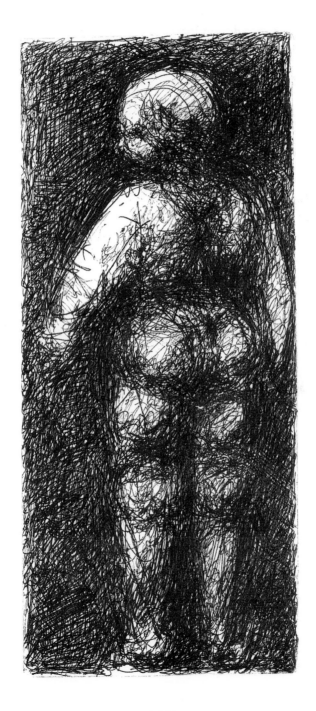

It was also clear to me that, unlike the nurse, my mistress enjoyed my role as both son and daughter.

With these thoughts in mind, I reported to the cook, Ellen, a large, red-faced Irish woman with a hot temper and a big voice to match. I would have to cultivate her friendship in my role as daughter of the house. She looked me over, arms akimbo.

I smiled and curtseyed before her, ready for instruction.

"Well, child, I shall have to teach you much, for I see that you are ignorant of domestic service. Nurse Sally is out there waiting for her soup. She's very particular about manners, so carry this bowl of chicken soup in both hands on the serving plate. Approach her from the left. Take the bowl in your left hand and very carefully place it before her. Then step back and wait till she has finished drinking."

"When she has finished, approach, always from the left, and indicate that you are ready to serve. You do not speak out loud because you must assume that there are guests and conversation must not be interrupted."

"When she signals, you may remove the bowl, which you will return to me. Do you understand, child?"

"Yes, Miss Ellen, I understand and thank you for teaching me."

"Well then, go. What is your name, child?"

"My name is Rose, Miss Ellen."

"Very good, now go."

I genuflected and turned carefully, walking on my high heels through the pantry door. I breathed a little prayer that all would go well and proceeded to serve my nurse Sally.

Sally indicated her approval, confident that the cook was watching. I stepped back and waited while Nurse sipped from the spoon, taking delicate bits of bread and butter. She was in no hurry.

When at last she was finished, I carefully approached as directed, took the bowl in my left hand, and departed from the room.

I Serve Dinner

I looked imploringly at Miss Ellen for approval. She was noncommittal and indicated that I should place the bowl in a pan of soapy water in the pantry. I did so and followed her into the kitchen.

"Good enough, child. Now the meat course. You will first place this empty plate before Miss Sally. Then return with the meat platter and hold it firmly with both hands so that she may serve herself with this fork."

I accomplished this task and returned to the cook for the potatoes, and in another trip, brought the string beans, which I returned to the side board. These dishes I now covered. I returned to my nurse and attended while she ate most delicately.

When all was eaten, I offered the meat for a second helping, which she refused. I then proffered the steaming vegetables which were also refused.

I returned to cook with the platters, then served dessert and coffee.

Having completed this lesson in service, I returned to my nurse and awaited further instructions. I was enjoying the slow ritual and dance-like movements of serving at table. I intended to learn my lessons well.

"Well, little Rose, I am pleased with your first lesson. You will need further experience because your mistress does considerable entertaining. Your movements from guest to guest must go unnoticed. Remember that you are only a servant and part of the furniture: Lovely, yet deferential."

"Now, let me look at you. Smooth out your apron. Come here, I must adjust your cap. Just wait till we can make you pretty with cosmetics and remove the veil."

"Well now, you may hold my chair when I rise from the table and then return to my lady to announce that dinner is served. Meanwhile, remove the napkin, replace glasses and utensils, and report to the cook."

Back in the kitchen, Miss Ellen said: "Now, my child you must stand at attention beside my lady's chair and assist her in sitting at the table. You only touch the chair." Then she dispatched me to the parlor where my Lady awaited.

"Dinner is served, Madame," I announced in a subdued voice, and escorted my lady to the dining room.

I went to my Lady's chair and there stood smiling, ready to serve. My Lady indicated her pleasure in my appearance, allowed me to seat her. She put her napkin in her lap and sipped water.

Noting that I was dismissed, I made a dainty genuflection and hastened to Cook.

"Now my child, your mistress will assume that you are tested and competent. She will ignore you as a menial and accept your services as expected. Do not be nervous. Delight in this glorious service. I think we shall get along if you are always careful for your lady's contentment. Now, bring the soup."

I made my reverence toward this great artist and proceeded to serve the soup. All went well and I was filled with joy. My lady seemed to enjoy her dinner and I emulated the patient furniture in my service. She accepted my service without comment and retired to the living room and her seat at the couch.

While she was absorbed in her book, I removed the eating utensils and returned the table to its former emptiness. Cook dismissed me and I put out the lights in the dining room. Taking up attendance on my lady, I stood behind the door in the shadows.

I do not know how long I will be occupied. My only hope is that I will always give Madame pleasure.

I Serve Dinner

I Serve Dinner

CURBING THE MANLY NATURE

After my lady tires of her reading, she looks up to see me patiently awaiting her pleasure.

"Come here, little one. I now wish to take note of your boyish nature which I intend to bring under my command."

At this, she rings for my nurse and commands her to remove my blessed female attire and return me to her in my page's attire. I am whisked off to be divested and returned to my basic attire of hose, body suit, and wig. When I am returned to my mistress, I can see that she is now intent on some form of discipline. My nurse flings me to the feet of my mistress where I lie in fear of her wrath.

"My child, you will now learn to curb any devilish desires for freedom from service at my command. Sally, get me the muzzle and fix it firmly over this manly child's pretty face."

Sally goes to a cabinet and returns with a kind of harness of silken black ribbon which she fits over my nose, around my brow and over my wig. The brow piece ties at the back; then a sort of muzzle is fitted over my mouth and secured at the nape of the neck, sealing my lips shut. Other ribbons seal my nostrils, and one which passes over my nose is stretched through a loop under my chin. My nose and mouth can thus be closed by pulling on this long leash.

This done, my nurse ties a sort of jacket around my body, effectively binding my arms tightly to my sides. She commands me to rise from my kneeling position. I cannot use my bound arms and I have to push myself up, using my head as a third leg. After much difficulty and heavy breathing, I succeed. Anklets are secured to my legs, connected to one another with a brass chain.

Curbing the Manly Nature

Muzzle Snuffle

I am now ready for the curbing of my manly nature.

Sally gives the leash to my lady mistress, who rises from the couch, a whip in hand. She pulls steadily on the leash, cutting off my breath. I am forced to move forward, shuffling in my fetters and delicate slippers.

Thus I am conducted to a ring attached to the wall six feet above the floor. The leash from my muzzle is tied to the ring so that my chin is elevated. In order to keep my nostrils and mouth open to breathe, I have to stretch up on my toes. I stare anxiously at the wall, unable to see what is taking place behind me.

Suddenly I feel the sting of the lash on my buttocks and legs and thighs. I am whipped until tears run down my cheeks and sweat drains from my body. Yet the pain is offset by a pleasing warmth which spreads over me, my mind gaining an astonishing clarity.

After thirty lashes, I am nearly exhausted and gasping for breath. I am crying with pain and fear, my knees buckling. I am given a moment to regain my footing, weakly trying to stand on tip-toe to gain oxygen, but can not, and fall into darkness.

The boy was seen to be hanging from the ring and in danger of asphyxiation.

"Take him down gently, Sally. I fear we may have to bring him around with ammonia."

The boy fell to the floor, a limp body, and was quickly revived with smelling salts.

"Remove the muzzle, Sally, and let him rest. Roll him in a blanket. He may be in shock."

The boy was led away to be prepared for bed.

Curbing the Manly Nature

Young man being prepared for marriage

TO BED

he boy recovered gradually under the competent ministrations of his nurse. Yet he was pitifully weak and so was conducted upstairs where he was bathed and perfumed as before and dressed in a voluminous night gown with great sleeves, skirts to his ankles and a ruffle about his neck. The serving cap was removed and was replaced by a pretty night cap which fit over his wig.

Thus he was conducted to a great handsome bed chamber and tucked into a four-poster bed and given some wine to drink. Sally sat by his bedside until, in spite of his wounds, he fell into a deep sleep.

He awoke with the sunlight pouring in from the dormer window and turned over. To his surprise, he found he was not alone; someone was sleeping by his side. He was too weak to see who it was and simply fell back exhausted.

He thought about his frightening adventures of the night before and wondered why he had been so punished. Certainly he was here to learn his duties as both son and daughter of the house. But he marveled at his voluminous night gown, the silken sheets, the soft blanket, and the great bed. He loved the morning sunlight. Reflecting on his intense experience of the day before, he then rejoiced in his role of service and even loved the experience of bondage, his face enclosed in netting and a bridle of ribbon under the command of his mistress and good nurse.

His bed companion, whom he supposed to be his nurse, stirred, rolled over toward him and threw an arm over his chest. He lay very still, eyes closed, awaiting his next adventure in this new life as a slave.

The unknown lady then sighed, took his head in her hands and kissed him on the mouth so hard that he thought he would faint.

The great breast enveloped him. He was certainly having a thorough education in the feminine culture and he was prepared to drown in it. The lady stirred again, and then, giving him a pat, rose and disappeared into the bathroom. He lay quietly, overwhelmed by a feeling of lassitude, awaited the return of his bed companion. He thought, with some apprehension, of his own family, father and mother and older sister Mary. How would he explain his disappearance and how was he to reconcile family life with his commitment to slavery? The thoughts were too painful and he resolved to leave the solution to his wise mistress.

Presently the lady emerged from the bathroom in a beautiful rose-colored bathrobe, smelling of lilac. She was none other than his great mistress!

Overcome with embarrassment at having shared her bed, he rose and knelt before her in confusion and buried his head in her skirts.

"Come, child, you must pull yourself together. All is well and you must bathe again and resume your life with me, your loving mistress."

Thanking her for her kindness, he sped to the bathroom and the toilet, closing the door. His great night dress and his collar and wig gave him some trouble, til he untangled the barely familiar garments.

Emerging from the delicious shower, dripping wet and naked, he was confronted as before by nurse Sally, who toweled and powdered and perfumed him with attar of roses. She restored his wig and night-gown and added a rose-colored dressing gown. His feet were covered in soft bedroom slippers and his scrotum was bound tightly in a silken under-garment closing at his waist. Nurse Sally was firm and sure in handling his private parts so that he was not allowed to do a thing for himself. His wig was covered with a pretty head cover and he was allowed to see himself in the bathroom mirror.

It occurred to him that his natural manly condition was to be completely supervised. There seemed to be no adult male life in this household. Only as a woman would Rose be treated as an adult and with the respect due a servant. As a page boy he would be tolerated solely as a slave. The feminine seemed to be his only outlet for freedom from control.

Rose was led out of the bathroom and found his mistress already seated at the window at a table for two. Nurse directed him to his goddess where he knelt briefly to be kissed. Then he was seated across the table from his lady. A bib was tied over his gown and so he was left alone with Madame.

Sally returned with a rolling caddie. She set the table with a cloth and two places and then served a breakfast of cereal, toast, jam, coffee and orange juice. Madame smiled at him but made no move to eat, testing whether he would wait for her.

Presently she spoke.

"Dear child, you are indeed my sweet companion. See how the sun has blessed us. Are you feeling well this morning?"

"Oh my mistress, you are so kind to your awkward child. I am really quite overcome with the blessings of this place. Yes I am, though I still feel the stings from my punishment."

"Yes, child, I shall explain to you the meaning of that episode. You must understand that in this house all things feminine are blessed, all things masculine are bound in slavery. You will learn to accommodate yourself to this condition of existence. I shall have a use for your manly nature but you shall find it confining. On the other hand you shall flourish as a little daughter or serving maid. In both these conditions you shall enjoy my passionate love. You must accept all these ministrations with all your heart and know that your mistress loves you with a jealous desire."

To Bed

At Table

He put his palms together under the fluff of his puffed sleeves and wristlets and bowed his head in reverence.

"Good child. Now we may eat this delicious breakfast which Nurse Sally has put before us. Mind that you don't spill anything on your gown."

She poured his coffee and her own and smiled upon him.

Rose observed that she handled the cup and the food with the tips of her fingers and took only little sips. She chewed silently and knew how to keep her sleeves away from the table and food. He observed all her actions closely and imitated them.

"I have a plan for us today, little Rose. Sally will dress you in a pretty little Eaton Suit and you shall learn to be my darling page boy and wait upon me so that you become familiar with the formalities of this house. Does this please you, child?"

"Oh, my mistress, my wise goddess. Your child is in heaven and longs to give you pleasure. My manly nature is curbed and my only will and desire is to serve and give pleasure. I have lost all desire to make choices. Give me what you will, command me. I put my trust in your infinite wisdom."

"Very well, then. We shall have another cup and then I shall turn you over to your nurse who will prepare you for this day's adventure."

Together they sipped in silence and unaccountably Rose felt his penis rise in anticipation of the training he should receive that day.

To Bed

Ecstasy

PAGE BOY

hen my nurse returned with the caddie, she removed the breakfast things and the table cloth and rolled the caddie out of the room. My Lady signaled to me to rise and help her up from the table. I stood at her chair and assisted her, kissing her hand. She expressed her pleasure at this spontaneous expression of devotion and did not scold me for taking this liberty. Perhaps I should be punished later. This was to be the day of the page boy and I could expect chastisement in the passion of my mistress.

Sally returned and took me in hand, her abject charge, her mistress' pet. She led me from the room and conducted me to a dressing chamber where I was to find all my pretty clothes neatly hung in the closet.

I found myself in the bedroom which I recognized as the one in which I had first been prepared and had lost my men's clothes. Unceremoniously, I was deprived of my night gown and bonnet. Sally then pulled black nylon stockings tightly up my legs, adjusted my scrotum high in the crotch and drew the waist as far up as it would go. Again she felt my crotch to make sure that the flesh was comfortable.

Over the stockings was drawn a short black cloth body-suit with silk lining that rose to the neck in the front and laced at the back. It crushed my ribs and contracted my waist as far as it would go. Again my private parts were felt and lifted by her powerful fingers.

The pressure between my legs was somewhat painful and I gasped for breath.

A shirt extending only to my chest was adjusted over this body suit. It buttoned in front. An Eaton collar was attached by a gold collar button, front and back; a great flowing black silken tie flowed

Page Boy

Dancing page boy in crepe de chine blouse,
white gloves and wig, white hose and black slippers with three inch heels

through the collar. Then I was fitted into a vest and a black cloth Eaton jacket which was tight under the arms. The coat only covered my ribs. A silken cravat was tucked under the Eaton collar, drawn tightly and tied with a great bow which covered my chest. Gray silk gloves were slipped over my hands and buttoned at the wrist.

When all was in place, gold cuff links were fastened to starched white cuffs, binding them tightly to my wrists.

"Now my child, comes the final test." So saying, she drew onto my feet black slippers with such high heels that I recoiled in terror at the thought of walking in them.

"All right, little one. We will now see what we can do about standing in your new slippers."

Forthwith, my nurse took my hands and lifted me from the chair, supporting me, as I found myself on tip-toe. Carefully she guided me to a full-length mirror at the wall and held me by one hand.

"Now, remember child, you are to concentrate on your heels for support—not your toes. You are to bend your ankles so that the forefoot makes an arch and your heel will form a platform on which to rest your body. I will not allow you to bend your knees. Your legs must be stiff as you stand and walk. Do you understand, my little Rose-bud?"

"I hear you, dear Nurse, and shall endeavor to comply, although I find it painful."

"Have confidence, little one, and depend for your balance on the strong grip of my hand. I shall be with you at all times when you are in those lovely slippers. The bow at your ankle will prevent your foot from sliding to your toes."

I balanced in my heels and endeavored to straighten my knees – a difficult task – but thus balanced and supported by my good nurse, I looked up into the mirror. I noted that I had a new wig with a boyish bob, very pretty, and that my suit was indeed that of a little scholar. My midriff was exposed. My black stockings were beautiful.

"How do you like your appearance, little one? This vestiture is the true garment of a little page serving his queen. Now essay a little curtsy. Balance on your right leg and put all of your weight on the right foot. Now step back half a foot with the left and put it behind the right."

I complied as best I could, barely succeeding.

"Keep your knees together and bow slightly."

Oh, I thought, I shall have trouble with this. And how long can my poor feet endure the strain?

"Never mind, you have much time to perfect this practice. Now let me return you to the chair. I need to restore the veil which enhances your beauty."

So I was returned to the chair and felt instant relief from the pain in my distorted ankles.

Again my face was covered with the finest netting and the veil adjusted under the chin. The ribbon was tied at the back of my skull and nape of my neck.

"Now your attire is complete as my little mannequin, the only kind of male allowed in this house. You must understand that you cannot have the freedom and strength of the male sex, but must ever be the little child of your great mistress. See that you do not disappoint her. Otherwise you shall be punished as you were last night; not for doing wrong, but rather to remind you of your total dependence in this house. Do you understand me, child?"

"Yes, dear nurse, I understand you very well and am determined to be worthy of this honor and condition of servitude," I replied with feeling.

"Very good, my little man, now we must make some practice steps. Rise, please, and get your balance."

So I rose on my heels and pointed my toes, clinging for support to my nurse.

"Oh dear, how it hurts."

"Never mind, you will gain such skill and confidence that you will miss the joy of this sweet elegance when you are allowed to walk in flat shoes."

Behold

Page Boy

Young servant adjusts his hose before presenting himself for service

PAGE BOY SERVES
THE GUESTS

he nurse guided the terrified boy to the living room and presented him to her lady mistress, who was settled on her couch. His steps were mincing. He stood stiffly and made a slight genuflection. Madame observed the discomfiture of the boy and indicated to the nurse to lower him onto the couch beside his mistress. He was terribly relieved to rest his feet but remembered to keep his feet and knees together.

Madame drew him to her breast and kissed him and told him he had been a good boy and that he only needed to practice and he would be a great pleasure to her at all times. "We'll rest a bit, dear, and then try again to do some little things for me. Later you will take a little nap and so be ready to serve some ladies who are coming to tea. You will be charming just as you are."

"Oh, dear," thought the boy, "what is to become of me in this guise? Well, I can only trust in my mistress. I am her servant." He breathed silently in the embrace of his lady.

In time, Madame ordered his Nurse to lay Rose on another couch, shoes and all, and let him rest there. At first he dreams, a dream he has had over and over since his youth.

I am in a small dark cell where I live and am safe and warm. In order to get food, however, I must leave the cell by going through the only exit, a tiny keyhole. In order to pass through this keyhole I must painfully transform myself into a tiny bug. This movement from one state to another is excruciating, traumatic. It is a submission, a destruction of the self which is absolutely necessary for my survival.

In my dream, I must do this several times a day, passing through the keyhole to the outside world, transforming back into a man on the outside. Then I must return to my cell, painfully squeezing myself into a bug to return to safety. It is horrible to think about, but it is absolutely necessary.

Rose awoke in panic to think that he had been sleeping when there was so much to do.

"Oh, my lady, I have been sleeping. I must rise and prepare myself for service."

"It's all right, my child, there is time to practice your steps. But now you will assist Sally in preparing the tea and arranging four chairs. Later, Sally will show you how to receive the guests at the door. So go to Sally now, my dear and follow her instructions."

So the boy rose carefully, smoothing out the silk cover of the couch and presented himself to his Nurse. He made the usual little reverence that was expected as a token of his submission and was led to the chairs in the corner of the room. Sally instructed him on where to place them. His mistress smiled at him from her usual place on the other couch. This done, he followed Sally into the pantry to prepare the tea caddie.

When these tasks were finished, his nurse led him to the foyer and initiated him into the proper way to receive guests, how to bow and then announce her arrival to his mistress. After several trials, he was tested to the nurse's satisfaction. Rose was told to wait for the guests at his station, an inconspicuous stool behind the door.

Rose obeyed and sat alertly on his stool, hoping that he should do well. He considered his condition of dress, and his very existence as nothing but the pleasure of another. The mistress will regard him with affection only to the extent that he pleases her with his beauty and sweetness of disposition. This is the musty enclosure of women!

Page Boy Serves the Guests

So he sat and was nearly slumbering when the bell rang. He opened the door and asked the lady her name and whom she wished to see.

"Why, you must be Rose. How pretty you are, child. I am Mrs. Wilson calling on Miss von Gunthardt. I am expected."

"Come with me, Madame. I shall announce you to my mistress."

He entered the parlor and with a genuflection announced, "Mrs. Wilson, Madame."

"Oh, my dear Grace, how lovely to see you again." Then, aside to Rose, "Very good, Rose. You may go now."

Rose bowed and returned to his post.

Again the bell rang and Rose admitted Miss Chilton, then a Mrs. Austen, and then a Mrs. Crain. All were seated in the parlor.

"That is all, Rose. You may retire to the pantry and serve tea."

"Yes, Madame," replied the boy and retired to the pantry.

The ladies all wore gloves which they removed and placed in their laps. There were no wraps. It was a mild day.

Rose found the tea to be ready, so he wheeled the caddie into the parlor before his mistress and stepped back, prepared to serve when instructed. The five friends stopped their chatter.

"Oh, Gladys, dear, the boy is beautiful. I'm sure he is making great progress under your fine direction," said the lady that he recalled was Miss Chilton. "May I touch him?"

"If you like, dear Martha, but first let him serve your tea. I think you like yours weak and with lemon."

"Yes, dear. How sweet of you to remember."

"Take this cup with the plate of cucumber wafers to Miss Chilton, Rose."

Rose obeyed reverently, but before taking the cup and plate, Miss Chilton pulled him close and felt his scrotum through the hose. The boy stood stiffly at attention during this rite and refrained from winc-

The Little Party

ing. He was surprised and shocked but knew enough to accept the conditions of his mistress.

"My! He is a man child indeed. And you know, he has a risen penis. How exciting."

"Well, Rose, what are you doing? Come, we have other ladies to serve."

The boy recovered from his trembling and handed Miss Chilton her tea and plate. After serving the other ladies, Rose was returned to Miss Chilton and was again felt and examined.

"Yes, he is pretty. Where did you get that Eaton suit, dear?"

"De Pinna carries them for St. Peter's School. I estimated the size and was fortunate to get a good fit. I'm glad you like it."

Page Boy Serves the Guests

His cheeks red under the face veil, Rose retired to the area beside the curtained entrance. He was indeed shaken but minded his own business.

The ladies talked of their own adventures with servants and all agreed that there was no substitute for an adopted child. After a while, his mistress told Rose to remove the tea and to prepare to serve dinner.

In the hallway, Rose paused to peer at himself in a hall mirror. He was not a little appalled at the vision of himself so utterly transformed into a sex attraction. He could not feel more naked; he was uncomfortable in the court attire, for it was tight and revealing and somewhat effeminate and he felt awkward in it. He was so corseted that he was forced to breathe from above his diaphragm. In short, he was not his own master. Yet when he contemplated himself in the mirror he also saw that he was wonderfully beautiful.

But he must not be seen thus taking note of himself or he would be punished for neglect of his duty; moreover he dare not contemplate too closely his lost manhood. Better to serve and love his mistress. So he hurried away to report as ordered, tripping daintily in his velvet slippers and practicing keeping his knees together as he walked. His penis was of course erect and bound to his abdomen.

When Rose arrived at the kitchen, Sally conducted him to a servant's lounge and dressed him as on the previous day in his pretty maid's uniform with the female forms strapped on below the dress and apron. His gray fawn-colored gloves were exchanged for white ones and the maid's cap was restored. His shoes were exchanged for the slippers with two-inch heels. He still wore the face veil that made his face nearly invisible.

When all was ready to Nurse Sally's satisfaction, he was given a pat on the buttocks and ordered to announce dinner.

"My lady, dinner is served," he announced with some importance.

"Well, ladies, let us enter the dining room and eat. We have a delicious roast beef and lentil soup."

While in attendance on dinner, Rose had observed that Miss Chilton was watching him with snake-like covetousness. Her gaze made him terribly uncomfortable but he knew better than to speak aloud in front of the guests. After dinner, his mistress and the guests retired to the parlor and Rose cleared the table. He knew that he should be needed in the parlor and took his place there. His mistress took note of this and nodded approval.

"Rose, would you bring in the card table and cards from the cabinet? Ladies, would you like to play bridge?"

Page Boy Serves the Guests

Miss Chilton demurred and said she would observe so that the mistress could play. The lady dismissed Rose and gave him a look of assurance. As the others played cards, Miss Chilton signaled for Rose to bring her an ashtray and then to light her cigarette.

"Stand beside me, child. I have need of you," she whispered, and seized Rose's hand in a grip as strong as that of his nurse. Miss Chilton drew him close and felt his calves and buttocks and scrotum with secret relish. He looked for help to his mistress, who was dealing cards. He sensed that he was being seduced and was in a quandary as to his expected deportment. Then he felt his scrotum being squeezed and stood trembling in the hands of this powerful creature.

Suddenly, he felt a great pain as this woman snapped a kind of clamp over his scrotum. The clamp was attached to a ribbon which when pulled tightened the clamp's hold on his delicate parts. Miss Chilton whispered to Rose that they should leave the party together for he was now her prisoner and her servant. If he cried out, there would be severe punishment. Miss Chilton quietly secured the ribbon to her chair out of sight of the other guests, and then rose to bid adieu to the mistress and the other ladies. She thanked them for a delightful visit and then excused herself by stating that she had an engagement for the evening.

"Oh, my dear Martha. I am sorry we could not include you in our game. Well, we shall be in touch, dear. Now, Rose, you will see Miss Chilton to the door."

He looked pleadingly for help but he was already dismissed.

Miss Chilton seized the ribbon from the chair and motioned Rose to proceed her to the door.

Rose obeyed this dragon lady, ensnared in her power.

ABDUCTION

ose opened the door for Miss Chilton, who gave a tug
on the ribbon. Poor Rose, nearly fainting with pain,
followed his captor down the stairs and into the night.
The woman hailed a taxi and shoved the boy in. She
directed the cab to a Broadway address in the Nineties.
Then she drew from her bag a muzzle which she fitted
to Rose's face and head, effectively preventing any cry for help.

Rose and his captor exited the cab unnoticed by passersby and
ascended the steps to a marble mansion. They were admitted by a butler and Rose was roughly thrown to the floor. Poor Rose lay sobbing
on the hall rug longing for his dear mistress, kind and dear as a mother, and was worried how she and Nurse must be concerned for him.

"Get up, child, so that I may teach you to forget your late mistress
and learn your duty to your present captor and ruler—myself. Get up
now."

What could the poor boy do but stagger to his feet and stand weep-
ing before this formidable creature, a terrible beast of a woman? His
leash was seized and he was dragged nearly blind and gasping for
breath and bound to a curtain rod, very strong, and there whipped, his
hands bound to his back. Oh, how the lash stung on his buttocks,
thighs, and back! There was no kindness here. He was to be used for
and at her pleasure, which was a fiendish delight in cruelty and control.

When he was freed from his overhead suspension he was conducted roughly by the butler to an upper bedroom and told to undress. He
obeyed with reluctance and placed all his dear clothing on a chair and
the slippers on the floor beneath. He kept on his wig and veil.

Abduction

No Escape

Then he was told to shower and prepare himself for bed. Gradually he cleaned himself and emerged from the bath refreshed, but in pain and apprehension. There was his fierce mistress, in her nightgown, prepared to take him in all his young manhood to be with her. She restored his muzzle and leash, pushed him into bed and tied the leash to the bedpost. Then she herself came to bed and hugged him to her breast with smothering grips. She slid his penis into her vagina, gripping his limp body with her strong legs. Thus he was held, his arms pinned to his sides, and kissed on the mouth. Overcome as he was with fatigue, the boy gave in to his impulse to serve and satisfied the animal craving of this great hungry woman.

In time, both fell asleep, he in her possession.

With the first light of dawn, Rose awoke and found himself with a slumbering woman. He realized this was his opportunity to escape. Very carefully, he slipped away from the great flaccid body and knelt on his side of the bed. He reached up, untied his leash and got to his feet. Gathering up his clothing, he vanished into the bathroom where he resumed his house-maid costume, including the female forms. He looked at himself in the mirror and arranged his hair. Slipping the maid's cap on his head and the apron under his dress, he carefully stepped out into the room. He stole down the stairs carrying his slippers. Unlocking the door, he emerged into the early dawn, a pretty girl for all the world to see. He was at Broadway and 96th Street.

"I shall walk back through the city to my true mistress and find my true home," he thought. "It will be a long walk and I have no money, but I must get home."

There were early morning idlers but fortunately he walked past them unobserved.

Many blocks later, he began to suffer from exhaustion and pain in his feet, but at last, happily, he arrived at his lady's house, climbed the steps, and entered the vestibule. He rang the bell desperately.

Abduction

No one came to let him in. Overcome with desperation and weariness, he sank to the floor and gave himself up to hope. He fell to dreaming that he was at the feet of his lady.

RESTORED TO FAVOR

e was awakened by Sally kneeling at the door and holding him in his arms. She had heard the bell.

"Come, child. You are a mess. The mistress has been so concerned about you. Come now into the parlor where she awaits you."

So saying, the nurse led Rose into the presence of the mistress and dropped the boy at her feet,

Rose looked up and trembled to note the wrath and disdain in her countenance.

"Well, child, I am not certain that I want you in my house after your desertion last evening with Miss Chilton. Do you hear? I am annoyed with you. Miss Chilton is a doubtful friend and quite capable of taking you from me. Tell me, did she charm you, child?"

Poor little Rose knelt in her black silk dress, head bowed under the stern regard of his enraged mistress. Dare he speak and tell his mistress the strange story of his entrapment? This would contradict the passion his lady had conceived against him. Perhaps it would be better to take his punishment as a foolish child, rather than to defend his reputation for loyalty.

"Oh, my lady. I return to you penitent and begging for reinstatement and forgiveness. Your servant is hungry and smitten with pain. See, I bow my head before the rage and indignation of my lady. Do with me as you will but do not abandon me. Oh, my goddess, have mercy on your humble servant."

"Well then, little Rose, we shall see if you are loyal and grateful for our kindness to you. Go now and clean up with your nurse, for you disgust me. When you are cleaned and fed, you shall be returned to

me and I shall hear your story. Take the child away, Sally dear, and clean her up and put her in a clean dress, for she shall remain female. When she is ready, bring her back and we shall learn the truth."

"Yes, ma'am. I shall prepare her and give her some soup and bring her back in half an hour."

So he was conducted to his little room and washed and restored to fresh clothing, a pretty pink gown, and led by the back stairs to the kitchen where he was given hot chicken soup and orange juice. Rose hoped that her nurse would mitigate the anger of her mistress.

"Well, now, my child, I shall return you to your mistress. Get up."

Rose obeyed, following his nurse to the great room and fell on his knees before his lady, who demanded an explanation of Rose's disappearance.

Restored to Favor

Kneeling as a supplicant before his mistress, Rose repeated the story of his abduction, his escape and his decision to return to his mistress. He knelt before her in his pretty silk dress, in humble submission, and awaited her pleasure.

After what seemed like ages, his mistress spoke again, this time in a softer, kinder voice.

"Well, my darling. Let me look at you."

With this she tipped Rose's leash up with the toe of her foot and so he looked up and saw her smiling, yes, even laughing.

"Little child, you must know that your adventure with Miss Chilton was by arrangement and was a test of your loyalty. You have passed the test. You have willingly returned to me, and I receive you back into my affection, for you are now truly my little daughter. Now I shall take you to bed with me and we shall both have some well-deserved sleep."

Then she took Rose into her arms and led him up to her bedroom. She undressed him and put him into his night gown and cap and into bed in her blessed arms.

So returned to favor, Rose fell into a deep sleep.

Rose awoke, his mind at peace, having been restored to the bosom of affection in this his true home. He lay still in the soft embrace of his dear mistress and determined to dedicate himself to her comfort, emulating the household cat, ever watchful, ever loving.

His sweet mistress planted a deep kiss on his lips and hugged him close, enveloping him in voluminous bedclothes and cap. He gave himself completely to these embraces, though he felt cramped and hungry.

"Come, dear. Sally will be here soon with a delicious brunch. Now, go to the bathroom and wash your face and hands. Be quick, my child."

When his lady emerged from her morning ablutions, he stood by her chair and seated her reverently, then took his appointed seat and folded his hands and watched her for the signal to pray.

There was a knock on the door and in came dear Sally with a great tray of luncheon foods. She poured the coffee and laid out the dishes, bread and butter and jam, eggs and bacon, orange juice. Rose observed that he was not required to serve this time but was treated as a daughter of the house.

When they finished brunch, his lady put down her fork and knife and commanded Rose to come to her and kneel.

"Very well, little Rose. Now I have another concern and that is to reconcile your absences from home with the concern of your parents."

"Oh, blessed mistress, you are so kind to read my anxiety at this point. I have resolved to leave this problem entirely to you."

"Very well, my child, tell me again about your home life."

"Blessed mother, my parents have no understanding of me or my sister Mary. Mary cares for me and is terribly unhappy under the moralistic authority of my mother. She is kind and loves animals and has a pet parrot. She is also artistic and loves to help unhappy people. However my mother's unloving control has stripped her of any ability to make her own decisions. She fears my mother and is indeed a prisoner in that house. Perhaps my lady could help her find a happy marriage and escape from this unloving control, for I believe that she will sympathize with my devotion to a loving mistress and will be your friend. Under your true guidance she would be your ally in keeping any secret."

"I find this information most helpful, child, and shall plan accordingly. I anticipate receiving your unhappy sister and sheltering her from abuse and strengthen her so that she may strike out for her freedom even as you have done. You must indeed return to your parents with an adequate explanation of your absence. I am aware that great pressure will be put upon you to stay at home and your parents will try to keep you there to cultivate your manhood. However, you shall find that I, your mistress, will take no chances of losing her pet. I have the means to keep you constantly reminded of your duty to me: You shall have to bear a constant reminder of your vassalage. Are you ready for this, my child?"

"Yes, my lady. I shall rest on your wisdom, for I am absolutely yours to keep."

"Well, then. You must return to your nurse and she will prepare you."

At this, Rose was dismissed and ordered to report to Sally in his dressing room.

Sally had laid out all of the manly clothing that Rose had worn in his former life as Gerald, the clothing that had been removed on his first visit to this blessed heaven. Rose washed and removed his pretty wig, now fully naked in front of his nurse.

"Now, my dear child, I shall give you the binding that will ever remind you of your service to your mistress."

With that, she bade him put on his jockey shorts. Then she sheathed his legs in nylon panty-hose and secured them to a tight belt strapped around his waist. To the belt she attached a kind of suspender which passed over each shoulder and through the belt at his pelvis. This done, she moved the cord down to his thighs, looped it around his legs and tied them into a tight knot high up his thighs near his crotch. She felt the scrotum and was satisfied that all was smugly bound. Then he was permitted to don his trousers, manly shoes, button-down shirt, jacket and tie.

When all was complete, he viewed himself in the mirror. To all outward appearances he was now an elegantly dressed young man. Yet he could feel his bondage under his clothes. He felt sufficiently bound at his waist and crotch and knew that he would be guided by his lady's wisdom in all the difficult encounters with his family.

Thus restored to manhood, he descended to the parlor, feeling strangely awkward in his low-heeled shoes. But the reassuring pressure of the stocking and the cord around his legs was familiar and comforting.

He presented himself to his lady and knelt before her for her blessing.

"Now, my dear, you will never forget your link to myself and will be guided in your deportment.

"You will present yourself to your lawful parents as a dutiful child, cheerful and confident and will reveal to them that you have found a wonderful mentor who will make you strong and wise. Assure your parents that they will ever find you loving and faithful. Now go. My love be with you and guide you. You shall return with your poor sister whom I shall love and educate, as I have done you."

"Yes, my lady. I think I understand, and thank you from the bottom of my heart. I am ever your loving servant and daughter."

"Well and good. Go now, my child. May you prosper."

He got to his feet and kissed his lady's hand. Sally showed him to the door which closed behind him.

Rose looked about at the crowded street and passing automobiles. He was enjoying this moment of freedom but knew that he would happily sacrifice it again in service. Rose recalled his other name, Gerald Graham. He walked as in a dream.

END BOOK ONE

Proud Servant

A SELECTION
OF DRAWINGS
WITH TEXT

I

Beautiful young page asleep in his mistress' couch. He is handcuffed and ankle-cuffed before he knows what has happened to him.

The mistress looks at him to see if he comprehends his new condition of total dependence. What a situation! There appears no means of escape.

The woman is amused by the boy's confusion.

"You must understand, child, that there was no difficulty in capturing you while you were asleep. Now you are mine – no doubt of it at all."

Malcolm is in service. He savors his skin-tight attire, which is light, delicate and revealing. He is the property of his lady. He falls to his knees and
crumbles before her as his Goddess. He rises and essays a delicate act of
homage such as might be repeated at every act of recognition or dismissal.
His costume will vary slightly in mood – sometimes they are light, loose
and graceful. Of course the shades vary like the shades of flowers. Some
costumes are for intimate evenings, for punishment, for errands, for play,
or for labor. Other costumes are for bedroom service, service at table, at
tea, or for the amusement of guests, for presentation, or for compliment of
his Lady's attire as a part of the entourage.

Enclosed in a woman's world with no escape.
"You're a disgrace and a shame to your mistress.
Where is your gratitude for all her kindness?"

Malcolm is presented to the lady guests
for their amusement at a tent in the garden.

This young page has paused on his errands to peer at himself in a hall mirror. He is not a little appalled at the vision of himself so transformed into a sex attraction. He could not feel more naked. But he must not be seen thus taking note of himself or he will be punished for neglect of his duty; moreover he dare not contemplate too closely his lost manhood. Better to serve and love his mistress.

So he hurries away to report as ordered, tripping daintily in his velvet slippers and practicing the touching of knees as he walks. His penis is of course erect and bound to his abdomen.

I receive special punitive discipline from
talked about. For the time being it is her pleas—
promise. Presently I shall be thrashed. Another
whipping. I sit on a bench trembling

overness I must learn to silent when
ture me and elicit favorable response
will administer the
her.

Book Two:

SISTER MARY

Book Two | *Sister Mary*

CONTENTS

ROSE VISITS
HIS PARENTS

ose stood before the familiar house of his parents. He climbed the steps to his house, took out his keys and let himself in. He found his mother in the parlor and greeted her as if his return was normal.

"Hello, mother dear."

"Why, Gerald! Where have you been? Your father and I have been so concerned for you. Why did you not inform us of your whereabouts?"

"Mother, dear, I have had a great adventure which I shall tell you about when father comes home. Please forgive me for causing you anxiety."

"Well, I shall be relieved to hear your story. Perhaps you will explain then why I should not disinherit you immediately."

Not wanting to quarrel, Gerald left his mother and went up to see his sister in her room where she was playing with the parrot.

"Oh, Mary dear. I have had the most wonderful adventure which I should like to share with you before I tell it to Mamma and Papa."

Gerald seated himself beside his sister, who was his senior by six years and took her hand.

"Mary, dear, I have come to realize how unhappy you are under Mama's constant supervision and scolding. I am ashamed that I have been unable to be a comfort to you. I am so young and inexperienced. Now I have found a friend who can help both of us. She is a beloved friend I visited last Friday. I want you to meet her; you will love her as I do.

"I have been living in her house and have become her servant. She understands my difficulty with approaching manhood and allows me

Rose Visits His Parents

to dress as a little girl. In that house, I would be your loving sister and so give you companionship.

"I know that things are so formal and controlled in this house that you feel like a prisoner. My new mistress is so wise that you will learn from her how to free yourself from Mama's bondage and find your own proper place as a person in your own right." Then Gerald paused and Mary responded.

"Why, Jerry my brother. How you have changed. You never supported me before and now you offer to be my brother indeed. What has happened to you?"

"Well, Mary. Let me explain as best I can what has happened. You see, this lady that I visited and met only the weekend before on a ski-train seemed to understand me better than I did. She knew that I was very weak in confidence. She took full possession of me and dressed me in serving clothes and disciplined and trained me in her service. I loved it and soon accepted her as my true mistress.

"For you it will be different, being a woman of twenty-six. You can come to her for sisterly comfort and guidance. She will give you strength so that you can defend your individuality and artistic nature. Let this be a secret between us and I shall bring you to her."

"Oh, Gerald dear," said his sister. "This is so frightening and yet, marvelous perhaps. She sounds even more formidable than Mama."

"Yes, but in a way that will help us to discover our true natures. We shall plan together how to arrange our escape. Meanwhile, I shall explain my absence to Mama and Papa at dinner. Till then, let me go to my room and rest."

In wonderment, Mary let him leave her room and returned her attention to the parrot.

In his room, Gerald silently prayed that the spirit of his mistress should guide him this evening.

Rose Visits His Parents

Servant and his mistress dancing together

THE CONFRONTATION

erald! Mary! Come to dinner." This was Mama calling.

Gerald hastily put on his pants and hurried down the stairs to report to Mama who was already at the table with Papa.

"Hello, Papa. I have come back late, but well and sound."

He kissed his father and took his accustomed place opposite his sister Mary. He braced himself for the somber meal ahead, remembering other miserable suppers dominated by his mother's wrathful words against his poor sister. Gerald's father had always silently supported his wife and seemed to despair of any harmony at home. Poor Mary had shrunk inside, in an effort to protect her individuality and lacked the confidence to oppose her mother.

Mother took charge during dinner, which was served by the maid, and after an uncomfortable silence, required of Gerald that he explain his absence, without communication, for three days.

Gerald felt supported by the bondage which he wore beneath his clothes and which symbolized his commitment to his lady mistress. He informed his parents that he had had the pleasure of a visit with a friend, who had offered him a home and the support he had never received from his own parents.

The mother tried to interrogate Gerald about his strange host but he refused to be coerced. Familiar threats were made about disinheritance and termination of college.

The Confrontation

Sister Mary was terrified and had no idea what should become of her if she were abandoned and put out of the house. But seeing her brother thus attacked roused her anger and she defied her mother.

"Your mother is right," father said weakly. "Children do have an obligation to their parents."

But Gerald faced him down and said that he, Gerald, and his sister Mary might leave the house together if Mama persisted in her cruel use of parental authority.

"Something has come over you, Gerald," Mama said, "and I mean to find out what it is. Where did you all of a sudden acquire the temerity to challenge your mother. This is monstrous. I don't recognize you."

Gerald did not respond to his mother but turned to his father and addressed him directly.

"I think you will agree with me that there is a strain between Mama's ambition for Mary and Mary's own bewilderment in the face of those, Mama's ambitions. You are, doubtless, shocked that your son should thus lecture his parents. Well, be not dismayed. I have learned that the weaning process is more painful for humans than for animals, and more painful for the proud than for the humble. The young need to help the parents in making this change. They can do this by exploring their own talents and inclinations, and thus assisting the parents in directing the training of youth.

"A wonderful friend has offered to help both Mary and myself at this crucial juncture in our lives. She supports and understands our innermost desires."

Gerald looked about him and found his father intensely interested in this discourse by his young son. Gerald did not look at his mother.

At this point, his mother demanded to know who this person was who presumed to take over the control of the two children of the house.

Gerald took his time answering this challenge, which he regarded as an interruption of a confidential discussion with his father.

"Mama, Papa, I understand that your question is reasonable from your past management of this household, but I also perceive that the question shows a deep distrust of the judgment of your children. Mama, your hold over your grown children is the threat of disownment and penury. You have not trained us in the world of business or in any field offering a profession; so breaking away becomes a decision requiring great independence and courage. Well, Mama, I now have the means for my escape from this prison of a home, and I mean to take Mary with me."

The Confrontation

Then, turning to his silent father, Gerald resumed in a conciliatory language.

"Papa, I give you assurance that you are not losing your children but gaining a powerful friend. Rest in your faith and know that all is well. You too, Mama, will learn to live with this emancipation and pursue your life of good works. Your children, who have always been a problem to you, will now be out of the house and on their way. You shall have word from them and an occasional visit, if you make them welcome. Tomorrow Mary and I shall bid this house and yourselves farewell. Goodnight, dear Papa and Mama."

So Gerald led his bewildered sister away from the presence of his astonished parents and ascended to bed.

Shaking from the strain of this experience, Gerald retired to his room, removed his manly attire and supports and had a good bath. Then, he carefully bound himself again in his black silk body suit, drawing the ribbon tightly so that he was aware his bondage. He carefully drew on his extra-long opaque hose and felt his crotch to see that all was smooth. Lastly, he tied his thighs around and lifted the draw strings to his waist band so that the thighs were stretched away from the crotch. Thus his scrotum was smoothly free from bulge right through to his anus.

He felt securely bound to his mistress and therefore to wisdom.

MARY JOINS THE MISTRESS' HOUSEHOLD

 erald arose at 7:30. He shaved, washed and creamed those parts of his body not bound. Then he dressed carefully and brushed his hair, which he sensed would some day grow and be formed into a pretty boyish bob. He brushed his finger nails and soaked them so that they were clean and well-formed. Tying his shoes over his nylon stockings, he found himself strong and ready to break free from the unwelcome bondage of his family. He led his tottering sister down to the door, carrying her bag. He left a letter on the settee in the foyer under the mirror and together they departed the house.

He hailed a taxi and they were driven to their new home.

Together, Gerald and Mary ascended the stairs to the mistress' house and were received by Sally. She led them to the parlor and announced that Rose had returned with his sister, Mary. The lady arose from the couch and greeted Mary warmly, taking the girl to her side at the couch.

"Dear Mary, I have expected you and arranged for your accommodation for a few days. My housekeeper will make you comfortable in a pretty room which will be yours. Please take a rest and at five we shall have tea together. I do so want you to be comfortable in my house."

"Mrs. von Gunthardt, you are so kind. I am terrified by the situation we have left with my mother, but am willing to try my brother's plan."

"Fear nothing. You shall be protected here and your mother shall learn, to her pleasure, that you have become a happy person. I asked

your brother to bring some samples of your flower paintings which he slipped into your bag. We shall look at them at tea. Now, rest and think happy thoughts, for this is a happy place. Sally will awaken you in time for tea. Till then, au revoir, my dear. We shall get along like sisters."

"I thank you, Mrs. von Gunthardt."

"Just call me Gladys, my dear."

Then the mistress showed Mary to her new room.

"Now, my little one," she said when she returned to Gerald, "you seem to have done very well. You will go to your room and prepare yourself as my little Rose and return to serve tea. Report here to me at 4:30. Meanwhile, clean up and rest."

Rose was left to prepare himself in the customary way. All his maid's outfits were laid out and he undressed with great excitement at the prospect of becoming a little girl again. How wonderful it will be to surprise Mary, he thought.

When bathed, creamed and perfumed, he resumed his female forms and wig and put on his dressing gown. He lay down to rest and dream of the beautiful life that would be shared with his sister and how she would prosper under the gentle hand of his mistress.

He arose at 4:00 p.m. and proceeded to dress himself with his wig and a bodice over the female forms. Fitting the veil over his wig and face, he smoothed his black dress and skirt. The apron and cap completed his service uniform. As he stepped into his high-heeled slippers, he felt so dainty and cute. He put on the silken gloves and moved before the mirror, practicing his little reverences and walking about the room picking up his men's clothing and hanging all in the closet. He was his own little maid servant again.

Satisfied that his appearance and his high-heeled walking were now correct, he descended and presented himself humbly before his lady.

Mary Joins the Mistress' Household

Looking him over, she indicated her approval and commanded him to report to Ellen in the pantry and prepare the tea tray.

At five o'clock Rose rolled out the caddie and entered the parlor where Mary and his Gracious Lady were conversing. He advanced and announced in a soft voice that tea was ready. His mistress said, "Very good, Rose. You may serve now."

As he rolled in the caddie, he noted that his sister did not recognize him and rejoiced that he was accepted as a house maid. He served the tea with a plate of cucumber sandwiches from which the crust had been removed. Then he stood back and awaited his mistress' sign. He overheard his sister inquire about her bother. Mrs. von Gunthardt explained that he had gone out to procure a newspaper.

How wonderful, thought Rose. I am indeed a household servant, perfectly trained.

"Oh, Gladys, you are so kind. I'm sure that Gerald is happy here. He tells me you met on the snow train to Montreal and that you were able to persuade him that you could help him to discover his true nature," said Mary.

"Yes, dear. I appreciate the lad's fine qualities, his sensitiveness and his sweet disposition. I am confident that he will do very well in his studies at Harvard and so please his parents. After college, I plan to send him to art school, where he will do very well. You see, I am quite rich and shall love to further his reputation as an artist. I understand that you also enjoy painting. Your brother has told me much about you and I understand that you love Italian people and their culture. I have Italian friends who shall become your friends, too. "

Despite the wonderful conversation, Mary kept referring to the absence of her little brother. The mistress seemed to realize that the time had come for Rose to be presented to her. But she would make sure that there was no change of role.

"My dear Mary, I know that you are concerned over the absence of your dear brother, Gerald, and I shall put you at ease about him. My little maid servant there is none other than your brother. You may observe for yourself the resemblance but I must require that you regard him as none other than my little maid servant. Do not speak to him as other than Rose, the parlor maid, and show your poise in playing the roles of mistress and servant without any reference to other relationships."

"Rose, dear, come here."

He obeyed and curtseyed.

"Now serve Miss Graham here a second cup of tea."

He obeyed reverently and ignored the inspection of his sister. He received her cup and returned it to his mistress. The Lady refilled it and returned the cup to Rose. Rose served his sister as an honored guest and returned to his station at the door.

Mary was speechless with awe and drank her tea thoughtfully.

"My dear, I think it best that you have no intimacies with my maid so long as she is in service. Do you understand me, dear Mary? This is a rule of the house. Rose will serve and you shall address her as my own servant Rose. She in turn will reject any other approach from you. I think you will enjoy the condition. Rose herself will report to me any violations of this rule."

"How strange, dear Gladys. Well, of course I shall comply and play my role. I know that you will do what is right."

"Very good, dear." Then, addressing the servant, she said, "Rose dear, you may now take away the tea and at 7:00 p.m. you will announce dinner."

Without a word, Rose removed the tea and returned to the pantry. Trusting his mistress to carry off the masquerade, Rose did her duty and addressed herself to setting the table and putting the pantry to

rights. He was delighted with the play and knew that his sister would respond and play her part.

Rose also knew that she would be severely punished if she transgressed the limitations of her station as a domestic servant by recognizing her sister. Moreover, he hated to disappoint his mistress in any way. So far there had been no opportunity for Mary to approach him. He would shun such intimacy and regard it as a violation of propriety to his lady if Mary attempted to communicate with him on a personal basis.

When the great clock in the hall sounded seven o'clock, Rose awoke to her duty with a start, quickly presented herself in the parlor and announced, "Dinner is served, Madame," with a little curtsy.

Mary was watching him and he studiously avoided her gaze, concentrating on his Lady Mistress whom he seated first. Then he seated the Lady Mary, as he would now think of his sister. Rose served the dinner while Madame entertained Miss Mary with stories of her life. Miss Mary seemed pleased to be treated as an honored guest after her years of treatment as a delinquent child. Madame complimented Mary on her intelligence and evoked an immediate response from the delighted girl.

Rose was of course delighted at this awakening of Miss Mary and studiously attended to her service, aware that his sister was watching him. Rose adored his menial position and his silken dress and had no time for any covert sign to Miss Mary. What a delight it was to serve! What more could he desire in life than this ecstasy!

After coffee in the parlor, Gladys said to Mary, "Well, dear young lady, we shall enjoy our day together tomorrow even as we have this evening. Rose will see you to your room and be ready to bring you whatever you wish. She is an excellent lady's maid."

"Thank you, Gladys. I shall gratefully go to bed, then. Oh, you are so kind!"

Then Miss Mary and his lady embraced with a deep feeling of love.

Rose stood waiting at the hall door and silently led Mary up the stairs. Miss Mary surprised Rose by patting his buttocks in a mischievous moment as she entered her room, but Rose took no notice and proceeded to turn down the bed.

"Is there anything more I can do for you, Miss Mary?"

Mary sufficiently recovered her poise to answer. "No, Rose dear. What a pretty maid you are, dear!"

Rose made a little reverence and said, "Thank you, Miss. If you wish for service, just ring this bell."

With a deep reverence, he backed out and closed the door.

Rose reported to his mistress and was instructed as follows:

"Tonight, my dear, you shall sleep alone in your room where you will be available to respond to Miss Mary's ring should she desire service. I think she will sleep well tonight. Now remember, child. Here you are a menial servant and know your place. Avoid any private conversation with Miss Mary. Do you understand? You can easily upset my plans for both of you if you fail me in this."

"I understand, my lady, and will be most respectful to Miss Mary at all times."

"Very good, Rose. Now you may remove the coffee and clean up the dinnerware. I shall remain up for a time and will ring for you when I need you."

"Yes, my lady."

As Rose departed, he thought to himself he had never seen his sister so radiant. She was enjoying this whole pantomime.

MARY IS GIVEN A LESSON IN COMMAND

he next morning, the Lady Gladys informed Mary, "Now we must do some planning for you, my dear. I think that you have a special gift for making friendships. You shall therefore become my house companion, later my pro-tégé, and we shall breast the tide of the great social world at its most brilliant. You yourself shall shine in your own light. We must discover who you are, my dear, for you do not represent your mother. I want to stimulate your eager mind with university studies. We shall have a busy life."

"Oh, Gladys dear. I shall work and study and serve for you. May my talents prosper for you, dear. You have so much to teach me. Oh, to be your companion! What a delight! And my dear brother."

"Stop right there, Mary dear. We have not spoken of Rose, who is in my personal service as a menial servant. You are to play a particular role for me as a mistress of my household. All the servants will be instructed to take direction from you. Little Rose is a housemaid who has been trained to serve in the dining room and parlor. You are to command her as a servant. You have no brother. Do you understand me? We have all to play roles in this life. Rose was in my service when you came to this house. So she remains. Let there be no intimate communication between you other than as maidservant and mistress. You must play this part exactly, my dear. Be it understood that there will be no intimacies between domestics and mistresses. Have I your assurance on this score?"

"Why yes, dear Gladys. Of course I shall follow the rules of this house."

Discipline

"Very good, then. Now, to establish this relationship, let us start immediately. Come here, Rose!" she commanded.

Rose stepped forward obediently and presented herself for service.

"You called, my lady?" she inquired with a reverence.

"Rose, it has come to my attention that you have assumed a certain special relationship to Miss Mary here. I have instructed Miss Mary that such intimacies are not allowed in my household between servants and mistresses. You are the most recent of my employees and must learn this rule of deportment. Do you understand me, Rose?"

"Yes, my lady. I shall be most careful in my future behavior."

"Very good, Rose. Now your mistress here would have some words with you. Go to her now."

Rose obeyed and did a reverence before his sister, standing attentively for instructions.

"Rose, dear, how long have you been in service?" asked Mary.

"Lady Mary, I have served here barely two weeks."

"I understand that your experience is limited to that of parlor maid and waitress at meals. I shall be requiring your service as my personal lady's maid. Perhaps Sally will give you some instruction. Will this be convenient, Miss Gladys? I should have inquired this of you."

"Oh, quite my dear. Do use the child," spoke Miss Gladys.

"So, Rose. I shall expect your service in my room when I ring for you."

Then spoke Gladys, "Now, Mary dear, since Rose has acknowledged certain infractions of house rules in the past, I think it wise that you chastise the girl so that the bounds of service be established forever."

Miss Mary seemed puzzled as to her next move, so Miss Gladys informed her of the whip hanging unobtrusively by the hall portiere.

"Rose, dear, you shall now procure the whip for me so that I may administer necessary punishment for your transgression," said Mary.

Mary is Given a Lesson in Command

"Yes, my lady," said Rose and quietly obeyed. She knew that Miss Gladys was observing this procedure with personal interest. Recalling her role in previous punishments, Rose fell to her knees before the lady Mary and bowed her head.

With apparent reluctance Mary raised the whip.

Lady Gladys said, "Mary do your duty. This servant must pay for serious offense against your own authority. This cannot be tolerated. So strike!"

Rose sensed the impatience of his new mistress and secretly prayed that Mary would do a proper job of it, for he was haunted by shame that he had so forgotten his station as to speak as a brother to this lady, his sister and mistress of the house.

Mary gently whipped the maid, to Mistress Gladys' disgust.

"Mary, dear, if you do not do a better job of chastising this servant, I shall fear to commit Rose to your service. Now stand up, Mary, and lay on so it stings. The child is waiting for this justice at your hands."

Poor Mary begged to be relieved of this fearful obligation so strange to her gentle spirit.

Miss Gladys arose in a rage and seized the whip from Mary's faltering hand and administered a blistering whipping that nearly caused Rose to faint.

"Do you understand my meaning now? Do your duty. I want this servant to know absolutely who is mistress and who is slave here."

Mary perceived that she was indeed being tested. So, taking the whip, she learned to crack it over the back and buttocks and legs of her prostrate brother, now her slave. In desperation, she whipped with increasing skill while Miss Gladys urged her on.

Nearly blinded with exertion, Mary collapsed in her chair and handed the whip to Miss Gladys.

"I see you have difficulty in establishing our control over this untrained creature. Well, we shall have further occasion to strengthen your hand, Mary. You may now command Rose to return the whip to its place and go to seek Sally who will give him the muzzle. Rose will bring you this delicate sort of bridle and I shall teach you how to bind Rose's head in it. You shall do this yourself and we shall have daily classes till I am satisfied with your command of Rose."

"You may now issue the command."

Mary realized her own duty and ordered her humble servant to go and seek Sally and return with the muzzle. Quickly Rose got to her feet, received the whip from Miss Gladys and hung it up. Then, turning to her tormentors, she made a deep reverence and sped upstairs on her errand.

She looked about frantically for Sally without success and realized that her nurse would be in the pantry preparing dinner. In great confusion and breathing heavily, she descended again and made an apologetic gesture to the ladies as she hurried to the pantry.

"Oh, Miss Sally. Please help me to find the muzzle for I have displeased my new mistress and am to receive punishment."

"Ah. I knew you were in for it when I saw you with the lady Mary. The muzzle is right here in its box. Take it to the ladies now," said Sally.

So Rose took the veil and its ribbons in her gloved hands and rushed to Miss Gladys, holding out the instrument like an offering.

"Very good, Rose. Now, take it to Miss Mary and show her how to bind it over your face. When all is properly in place you will hand Miss Mary the leash."

Rose obeyed and showed Miss Mary how to smooth the veil over his face and fit the skull ribbon and tie it behind his head. The delicate netting was gathered behind the jaw, and the ribbon looped under his chin closed his nostrils and mouth. When Miss Mary had felt all around the maiden's face and head, Rose handed her the leash.

Muzzle

Then Miss Gladys spoke up and suggested that she bind Rose's wrists and ankles together with a one foot ribbon between them.

"Now, Mary dear, you have complete control of this your servant who will be given you to train as you would a puppy dog. This puppy has already been house trained and eagerly responds to the leash. Yet you have restricted his movements so that he must mince and hobble in following your lead. So be careful not to go too fast or Rose will fall."

Thus bound, Rose looked through the veil and bonds to her new mistress for leadership. Lady Mary was somewhat confused but took the leash and gently pulled. Rose lifted her chin in response and took a little step toward his mistress.

"Now, lead Rose around the room till you get the feeling of mastery. Why should you not enjoy this? Rose may be your pet to care for while in this bondage. You may keep her thus all night and love her as you would a little dog. Without the leash, Rose will be bound and subject to command like a servant."

So Mary led the pliant servant about the room and saw that the latter was in ecstasy.

"Now, my dear, you shall lead the child to your room and make a warm place on the floor at the foot of your bed, where you will bind the leash to the bedstead. There he shall sleep this night."

"And remember that Rose in the muzzle responds only to commands. Do not attempt any confidences with Rose for she is bound to house rules and will report to me if you transgress. Is this clear?"

"Oh, dear sister. I shall play the part of mistress and love my little pet who is so sweet. Thank you for teaching me all these things."

"In the morning you may unleash Rose and train her to care for herself and for you. Sally will come and help you then. So, my dear sister, take Rose to your room and do as I say. Sally will be there to help you."

Mary is Given a Lesson in Command

The Blessing

Mary led her little ward, holding the leash high, up the stairs, and to her room where Sally awaited her. Sally had already prepared a little bed at the foot of the great bedstead and now observed while Mary tied the leash and put Rose's head on a pillow. Rose looked up at her mistress in utter joy, and after being patted on the cheek, she gave herself to sleep.

MARY LEARNS TO TAKE RESPONSIBILITY

ith the early light of day, Mary rose and came to her little pet, and kissed her on the cheek. Then, finding herself alone, she removed the muzzle and took the child in her arms and loved her.

Then, overcome with confusion and some loneliness in her new surroundings, she said:

"Oh, Gerald, my dear little brother, how I long to speak with you. Where is Miss Gladys leading us with all this pantomime?"

Little Rose put her hand to her lips and silently pleaded with his mistress not to break the rules of the house. Then, in terror, Rose assumed an attitude of prayer and refused to understand. Mary cried and hugged her pet, wishing for protection herself, but Rose only remained passive.

"Oh, my dear brother, please let us plan together and think together. I do not understand this new discipline here. Why are you, my brother, reduced to a common servant, and I forced to play the part of your mistress?"

At this, Rose surprised Mary by standing up and cautioning Mary to stop this defiance of Miss Gladys.

"My dear mistress, I must report this to my lady Gladys immediately for I am her slave."

With that, Rose fled the room in tears, rushed up to Miss Gladys' room and knocked for admittance. She was permitted to make her submission to the great mistress of her heart and beg for protection from the appeals of the Lady Mary.

"My child, you have done well to report this to me. I shall therefore forbid Lady Mary to have you in her service. Go child, and get Sally and bring her to me."

Rose obeyed and fetched Sally to the mistress.

"Sally dear, it appears that Miss Mary does not wish to cooperate in my plan for her. You will therefore substitute for Rose as her servant and see that Mary is isolated in this house."

"She will dine in her room and be a prisoner. She shall learn that I am the Mistress here and that as a woman she too must learn to realize her power. You may therefore bring Mary her breakfast and serve her and forbid her to leave her room."

"Yes, my lady. It shall be as you desire. I shall assign Rose other tasks as parlor maid and there shall be strict surveillance of Miss Mary."

"Very good, Sally dear. I depend on you to maintain an orderly house for me. You may go now and take Rose with you." With that, Rose was conducted to the parlor and instructed in dusting and vacuuming the rug, and shaking out the curtains.

Mary was confined to her room and suffered from her isolation, almost regretting her decision to leave her parents and seek refuge in this house of slavery, this new prison. She cried and longed for her dear parrot, Alibaba, to whom she could unburden her fears and give her love. Despondent, she rang for Sally.

"Oh, Sally dear, how shall I survive in this cold house? Why am I confined to my room?'

Sally responded coldly to this weakness and quietly suggested that Mary think about her good fortune in finding a caring mistress.

"Miss Mary, I am instructed to serve your needs. You have not eaten your breakfast which is now cold. Could I bring you some books or some sewing materials? Your mistress will see you when you are ready to beg forgiveness for your breach of the rules. You have much to learn from the lady Gladys before you are ready to have your ways within the rules. I am afraid you are a lazy spoiled child and must bear your punishment for a while and learn that nothing is gained without sacrifice."

"Oh, dear, who can I love and who can love me? I perish here just as I did at home," said Mary.

Then Sally said, "Just quiet yourself. My mistress will not see you until you have learned self-control, as Rose has done. You have important decisions to make. I leave you now to meditate on your present condition."

So saying, Sally left the room to the disconsolate prisoner.

Poor Mary, what was she to do? It seemed that her brother was bound to his mistress and Mary was her prisoner also. But was it possible that Gladys in her wisdom was trying to put some strength in her weak will and save her from herself? Perhaps Gerald was acquiring this strength. He'd certainly displayed it during the confrontation with their parents.

"I think I must make my peace with Gladys and accept her guidance, however mysterious," she thought. She feared Miss Gladys, who was strong and assured. "Oh, what a weak creature I am."

So, with trembling, she opened her door, realizing that she was breaking her sentence of confinement. Seeing no one, she stole down the great staircase and entered the parlor where Rose was dusting the mantle piece and its ornaments. Addressing Rose as a servant, she inquired where the mistress was. Rose made a reverence and replied that the mistress had gone out. Mary decided to await her return at the sofa and contemplated the difficulty of her task in persuading Miss Gladys to return her to favor.

MARY ASSUMES RESPONSIBILITY

nable to sit thus awaiting her fate, Mary rang for Sally. "You called, Miss Mary?" Sally had come silently and startled her.

"Oh, Sally dear. I am terribly confused. I understand nothing and have decided to make my submission to Lady Gladys. Please help me. I am weak. How can I persuade Miss Gladys to take me back under her control. I promise to be good and obedient."

"Poor thing," said Sally with mingled pity and contempt. "You cannot benefit from my lady's wisdom unless you have absolute faith. How can she give you strength and purpose and resolution if you waiver in your loyalty?"

"Oh, Sally dear, I am a lost soul indeed and desperately need guidance."

"Well, Miss Mary, you have both the advantage and disadvantage of being a woman. The advantage is that you fit into the feminine condition of this house. On the other hand, my lady will require much of you as an equal. She will expect you to stand beside her and assist in her social and business affairs. You will be required to assume responsibilities in this house and give my lady confidence in your loyalty and ability. You have been spoiled by the easy life provided by your parents, whom you have disgusted by your weakness. You have no drive, no will."

"Oh, Sally, what do I have to offer of service? I feel so helpless and useless." With this outburst of feeling, Mary fell to her knees before this cold and unapproachable person.

Mary Assumes Responsibility

Tough Mistress

Sally stepped back with disdain and admonished the girl to get to her feet and behave in a manner suitable to her station. Continuing, she spoke:

"I am a servant in this house and demand to be treated as such. Now, stand up immediately and pull yourself together. How dare you so demean yourself before the servants! They will be confused and unable to obey your commands. See, now in the absence of my mistress, you alone are in command here as her deputy. As housekeeper, I can run the establishment, but do not assume command."

Mary rose and wiped her eyes and collapsed in the sofa, disconsolate. Sally left the room hurriedly to avoid dealing with this weak mistress, and so Mary was left to think about loyalty and strength and being worthy of the responsibility for the household.

A thought occurred to her. Why not test her mettle with this nurse and call her back? So she rang. Sally returned and again inquired what was desired of her. Mary sat up straight in her chair.

"Sally, you just left me without my permission. As you know such conduct is not tolerated in this household. I want you to apologize to me immediately!"

Surprised and delighted, Sally made a reverence and said, "My lady, I do apologize for my behavior in thus leaving your presence. I know my station and my duty. I accept the reprimand of my lady's mistress and promise never to repeat such irreverence."

"Very good, nurse. Now go about your business. I shall ring for you if I have need of further services."

"Yes, my lady," said Sally, and made a pretty curtsy. She departed contentedly, now that Mary had assumed her proper station as pro-tempore mistress of the house.

Mary sat quietly marveling at the change in Sally. A thought occurred to her. Why not exert some authority over Rose, still silently dusting the room.

"Rose!"

Rose presented herself.

"Have you finished with your dusting?"

"Almost finished, my lady," said Rose.

"I want you to fix me some tea and then go to my room and set all in order. When you have finished, I want you to change into your page costume and report back to me."

"Yes, my lady," said the maid with a pretty reverence, holding her skirts and stepping back with one leg.

Rose left the room and brought the tea, then ascended the stairs.

Mary Assumes Responsibility

Mary composed herself and began planning little services that Rose might do for her. Now, what can I think to do for Lady Gladys? she thought. Perhaps I can help her plan for the evening at the opera she talked about. I must now show my strength and loyalty. She resolved that she would greet her lady with great cheer and enthusiasm, ready to serve and learn her duties in this house.

Mary sipped quietly, enjoying the tea, when Rose entered in his page's livery and reported that his lady's room was in order.

"I have laid your clothing in the bureau and hung up your dress and put the bag on the rack. I have aired the room and vacuumed the rug and dusted. I trust I have pleased my lady."

"Very good, Rose. I shall see how well you have done later."

The bell rang. Rose begged permission to open the door. Mary deigned to grant it and watched as the maid departed. She heard Rose report to Madame that Lady Mary was awaiting her in the parlor. When Gladys entered, Mary rose and greeted her with a happy smile and inquired if all had gone well with her during the morning.

"Why yes, Mary dear. I am a bit flustered and am pleased to see you so happy. Very pleased indeed. Rose, I shall also have a cup of tea."

Rose departed on her errand.

"Well, my dear, I perceive a change in you. What has happened?"

"Gladys, dear, I confess that I left my room in despair and so broke my pledge to you. However, Sally has been teaching me command. I have indeed made a transition and have made a resolution to do all in my power to bring you satisfaction. I truly wish to be of help and only beg for your instruction."

"That is well, Mary. I am pleased with you though I was shocked to see that you had left your room against my orders. We shall go into that later."

"Thank you, dear Gladys. I have given Rose instructions to put my room in order, I have ascertained that Sally is counting the laundry and that cook has prepared lunch for one o'clock. Thus I have made a beginning of sharing your responsibilities in the management of this house."

"That is well. When you have learned how to relieve me of the household management, I can go on to my many assignments and community services.

"Mary, dear – I know that you have been frustrated and unhappy at home. It is my wish to restore you to creativity and happiness. It has occurred to me that you should go to Italy and study art. And you shall recover your natural beauty and health. You shall be loved and appreciated in Italy. If this pleases you, we can address the problem of presenting the plan as financed by a scholarship or grant. You see, I also have plans for Rose. Rose will let his natural hair grow and give it a boyish bob. He shall continue his female role while you are in Italy and then I shall provide you both with the means of beginning an art career here in New York."

Mary responded:"Oh, my dear Gladys! How wise you are! You see right through my misery and bring light into my darkness. My dear little brother was certainly fortunate to meet you. You understand his weakness and strength at the same time."

"Well, dear, we have ample time for our plans. Do not worry. We shall be happy sisters and little Rose will grow in his sweet service to both of us."

Rose heard all these plans for himself and Miss Mary and was transported with joy. So he should be allowed to remain a lady's maid and serve Miss Mary and his mistress. Oh, how grand it would be.

END BOOK TWO

Mary Assumes Responsibility

Young slave experiences his new badge of servitude, a permanent jewelled and spiked collar to which he must become accustomed by restricting the turning of his head.

A SELECTION
OF DRAWINGS
WITH TEXT

II

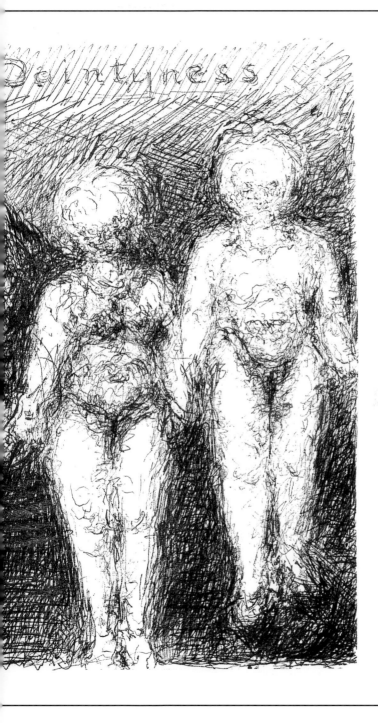

The perfect slave adores his mistress and submits cheerfully to her loving
indulgences. Here she tests his patience under her delicate punishments,
controlling his breathing by drawing the ribbons of his muzzle tighter, closing his lips and nostrils. If he faints, she will revive him and comfort him,
as she would a little pet. He kisses her hands and feet in an ecstasy of joy.
"Oh my little baby how I love you!" she says.

Young servant escapes momentarily from domestic confinement
to taste the freedom of salt air and sea water at a rocky shore.
May no one spy him and report!

Rouged Lips – Young man entertainer displaying his sex appeal.
Is he not charming in his ruff and hose and slippers?

I am chastised.

My little mistress is enraged at her page and knows her duty to administer discipline to me in her little household. I am instructed to go before into the garden bearing the whip. There I am told to bend over double and run in this position, hands clasped to my breast, while she follows behind whipping my back and buttocks and legs.

In this position and in my high-heeled slippers my movement is much restricted – not to mention the tightness of my bodice, so that I soon fall panting to the gravel pavement and so lie, receiving my punishment in the supine position.

When she is out of breath, my mistress flings the whip at me. I lie awaiting further chastisement, but she has gone away and left me. I retrieve the whip and return it to the desk beside the door.

Book Three:

RESOLUTION

My three personalities: Male, female and neuter

Book Three | *Resolution*

CONTENTS

ROSE HAS A TERRIBLE EXPERIENCE

ne day about a week later the Lady Gladys dispatched Rose on an errand to the Post Office.

"You must be quite careful to speak to no one. Sally will prepare you for your mission in the streets of New York."

Rose gathered up the envelopes in a rubber band and put away the card file and stationery. She put the envelopes in the pocket of her apron and ascended the stairs to report to Sally, who said, "Oh, my little lady. We shall now equip you in modest but becoming attire for your trip to the post office which is on Broadway and 66th. You will wear this dress, Rose. See, I have a little handbag for you and a summer hat and gloves. Let me remove the veil and study your make-up."

Sally stood before the great mirror and applied pancake makeup and rouge and lipstick and surveyed the effect.

"Now, put the letters in your purse. Let me see you walk in quick little steps, quite confident and purposeful. Go to the bureau there and pretend to do business. Now return to me. Of course all you have to do is deposit the letters in the slot for Manhattan mail. Should there be others before you, just stand prettily and quietly, keeping your feet together and your elbows in."

Rose performed as directed, stood as if waiting in line, and then returned to Sally with a little curtsy.

"All right, child. Be off with you."

Rose was given an affectionate pat on the buttocks and launched forward on her great adventure. She let herself out into the street feeling happy in her pretty new outfit and headed east toward Broadway.

Rose Has a Terrible Experience

Enjoying her female role, she felt the cool air on her stockinged legs and the rapture of her silken attire. She had grown accustomed to the shoes and managed pretty well by concentrating on her heels. Weight on the heels, she thought. Now I am a true girl!

Standing erect, Rose was determined to enjoy her altered sex. She took care to step down and up from the curbs. Passersby sometimes stared at her, but she looked straight ahead and so was allowed to continue on her errand. She looked at herself in a store window, noted that the veil over her face was nearly invisible, and rejoiced in her appearance. By now she had mastered the walk in high heels and felt so natural that she smiled at the passing women and admired the babies in carriages. Some workmen looked her over but she went on her way making light of their stares. Being a woman was such a joy in itself she could only pity them in their uncouth and tragic manhood.

At Broadway, Rose waited for the traffic light and hurried with the other pedestrians across the pavement. She tripped up the steps of the post office and stood in a short line before depositing the letters in the Manhattan slot. As she descended to the street, she confronted a young man who had been in Gerald's class at school. They stared at each other and Rose had to overcome a desire to acknowledge the friend of her former life. But she did not panic. Instead she walked purposefully past the puzzled young man and continued her way back to the house on Riverside Drive.

Being outside of the safety of her mistress' home could be dangerous.

Almost as soon as Rose had shut the front door behind her, the front door bell rang. Peering through the lace door curtains, she noted that the caller was in the uniform of the United Parcel Service and was carrying a package. Rose opened the door a little and told the messenger to hand her the receipt book and parcel so that she might take it to the mistress for her signature.

To her consternation, Rose found that the man was observing her closely – too closely for comfort.

"Hmm, let's see a little more of you, cutie. Just let me have a look at you."

With that remark, he pressed back the door and seized Rose about the waist and smothered her with kisses. Rose was overwhelmed and struggled to free herself from the man's grip. She called out and tried to escape to the safety of her mistress' home. Instead she found herself pulled outside where passing people gathered to see what the commotion was all about.

"What's this?" yelled the man. "Not a girl but a phony! You'll do for a laugh."

Rose found himself held by the horrible man at the top of the steps. He was exposed for the people to see. His wig was torn off and his clothing in disarray. Poor Rose stood in the midst of these howling males and in the grip of this jeering tormentor, his tears flowing copiously. Finally he heard a siren and presently, a police sergeant stood before them. He dismissed the crowd and threatened to hold Rose and his tormentor on charges of disturbing the peace. They were also prepared to arrest Rose, the exposed transvestite, whom they accused of indecent exposure.

"Oh, officer, please don't take me away. I am a servant in this house, where my mistress will answer for me. I beg you to return me to my mistress."

At this moment, all present observed the lady of the house standing in the doorway like a tigress, demanding an explanation of this monstrous treatment of her servant.

"Officer," she called to the police sergeant, "what is this violence and why are your holding my servant?"

The officer stepped forward and addressed the lady.

"Madame, it is my duty to make a full report of this person's indecent exposure. You say that this is your house and this is your servant. Perhaps you will permit me to enter your house and ask you some more questions. Thus I shall be more able to make a full report. "

"Of course, officer," said Madame. "I desire that you bring with you not only my servant, but also this villain in the uniform of the United Parcel Service. I intend to press charges against him for conduct unbecoming his position of responsibility, and for assault."

Arrested

Rose Has a Terrible Experience

Madame was magnificent in her rage and indignation, demanding the dispersal of the people and conducting the police and the prisoners into the house.

Rose and the cause of his trouble were both handcuffed and conducted into the house, following the lady into the parlor.

Standing before the police officers, Madame spoke as follows:

"Sergeant, I shall now introduce myself if you will take note. I am Mrs. Gladys von Gunthardt, widow and owner of this house. The person you hold in arrest is my servant, who, of his own free will has chosen to serve in female attire, a private matter between us. I do not give you my servant's real name, for he comes of a well-known family in this city and I must protect him from this unnecessary embarrassment, not of his or my making. It is I who shall press charges against this intruder, who has exposed the child against his will."

"My humblest apologies," the police officer said, cowed by her position, her wrath, her magnificence. "I leave you now to recover from this awkward incident, and thank you for your cooperation."

Thus, order was restored and the shaken Rose was allowed to retire to bathe and rest. After that terrible experience, he found a great determination to better understand the ways of being a woman. Certainly with more training at the hands of his able mistress and his newly powerful sister, he would finally learn the secrets of womanhood.

ROSE AND MARY GO SHOPPING

eeks passed in glorious service, Rose practicing on the walking machine at his mistress' pleasure, his hair growing long and lovely, his complexion and figure developing in his role as daughter.

One morning, Rose was attending his mistress when Miss Mary came down and joined Gladys on the couch. They greeted each other warmly and Miss Mary thanked Rose for her breakfast. Rose curtseyed in acknowledgment and stood quietly at the door.

Miss Gladys suggested that Mary and Rose go shopping together that day and enjoy their new station as sisters. Mary was to watch over her younger sister and instruct her in the ways of women.

Mary was delighted – they would go to Bonwit Teller and select some clothing and handbags and other accessories for Rose and herself. Miss Gladys assured her that she could spend freely from Gladys' account there.

Sally had laid out the prettiest pink dress for Rose to wear and rose-colored shoes and gloves to match. Rose delighted in her new finery and glowed with joy when she stood before her lady, who presented her with a lovely beaded bag equipped with some cosmetics, a hand mirror, a comb and a little change purse.

Rose was a little anxious about going out in public in her feminine clothes after her terrible experience with the UPS man, but the lady Gladys was reassuring.

"Rose, in the last few weeks you have truly developed into my young daughter. Your hair has grown, you have learned much in the

The Feminine World

use of cosmetics and how to walk. This will be a test of your femininity, and I am confident that you will pass.

"Now, my dear. You are now your sister Mary's little sister and you will learn from her all that a woman should know in the outside world. You will enjoy yourself and serve your sister carefully while she protects you. You will have perfect manners and should you meet any friends of your sister, she will present you as her sister, Rose. You will carry this bag on your left arm and keep your elbows close to your side. Now, let me see how pretty you look."

So Rose paraded before his lady and practiced sitting and rising daintily.

"Oh, my little darling, you are indeed beautiful. You must be careful not to look at men and stay close to Mary. Oh, darling, give your mother a little kiss! You are embarking on a great adventure as a young woman."

So Mary and Rose taxied to the Bonwit Teller Department store. Rose became separated from her sister in the surge of ladies in the jewelry department and looked about herself, somewhat frightened.

A gentleman came up to her and asked if he might be of service. He was tall and wore a black suit, quite elegant. Looking her over, he seemed pleased with her appearance. Rose blushed and begged to be left to her search. But the man stayed with her.

"Oh, my dear Rose!" called Mary. "I lost you for a moment. Who is this gentlemen?"

The man replied: "Miss, I perceive that you are this dear lady's sister whom she has been seeking. I was helping her to find you. She seemed quite overcome with anxiety. She is so charming that I could not leave her in her distress."

"Sir, my sister is on vacation from convent school and not accustomed to the attention of strange gentlemen."

"I see," he said, tipping his hat and excusing himself.

"Oh, my dear," Mary said to Rose, "do not be frightened by this stranger. You are bound to attract young men with your natural sweetness. Perhaps we shall arrange a little reception with Gladys' permission and you shall learn how to manage ardent souls. You will then learn the power of women to help such lonely males."

Rose and Mary Go Shopping

Rose thought to herself that her transformation into a woman was almost perfect.

"Now," said Mary, "let us pick out a pretty dress for you and something for me to wear to the opera tomorrow night."

With that, Rose proceeded hand in hand with her sister Mary to the dress department, where they examined some evening gowns. Rose was an inch taller than Mary and yet slender and very spiritual. It would be easy to find a beautiful gown for her.

Mary selected for herself an elegant long shift, and for Rose she picked a lovely blue chiffon creation with a delicate raised collar, and took Rose into the ladies' dressing room. Mary removed her sister's street dress and slip and helped her into the long night-blue slip and dress. She fastened the eye hooks at the waist and the puffed sleeves over the shoulders. After she fitted delicate white gloves over Rose's hands, she clasped a beautiful gold chain necklace under the chiffon collar. She selected little dancing clippers for Rose's feet and drew a delicate veil over her eyes secured at the hair.

Rose turned around in the dressing room, which was mirrored all about. She examined her own reflection and fell into a contemplative mood, feeling the sheath of filmy material falling like water over her legs. Her hair was long, her complexion was white and pink and soft; her whole body seemed to tingle with a new life. She felt the forms of her breast and thighs and waist, and how feminine they were.

"Now, my dear," spoke Mary. "I shall take a chair in the reception room and you will come forth from here as though presenting yourself for the evening guests to see. Our love shall give splendor to your beauty."

Rose heard Mary speak to Miss Carson, the sales lady, and ask that the lights be lowered and a word of introduction be spoken signalling Rose's emergence in her evening finery.

Miss Carson knocked on the door of the dressing room and inquired if Rose was ready to come forth.

"Oh, my dear," thought Rose to herself. "Is it possible that I am becoming a woman? Oh, I must let this moment work its ways. I feel so exalted. Yes, I shall come to Mary forever changed. This is wisdom!"

Rose awoke from her reverie seated at the dressing table before the mirror. Now she would be seen by all to be a beautiful woman. She arose and answered that, yes, she was ready. The door opened and Rose stepped onto the threshold and into the spotlight.

She stepped forward into the great room and let her hands fall to the folds of her skirt. Deliberately, she advanced to her sister and stood before her.

All was silence. This was the moment of her initiation into womanhood. Mary and the onlookers would bear witness to this magical transformation.

Rose knew she was a vision of moonlight, a delicate evening rose. The entire company of clients and sales ladies, and Rose's own sister who knew her, rose up in applause.

Rose, through meditation and in this dream,
becomes a girl, not only in dress and form, but in very fact

Rose and Mary Go Shopping

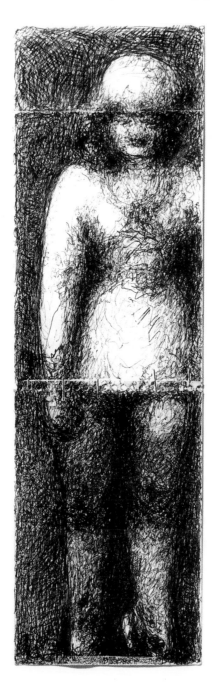

ROSE ALONE

hat evening the Lady Gladys was to take Mary to the opera, an Italian drama which she felt Mary would enjoy. So after dinner, Rose assisted her goddess in dressing. Her lady was truly an elegant queen, and Rose her humble servant.

Then Rose helped her sister into her new evening dress from Bonwit Teller. They descended the stairs, Rose proceeding delicately to the parlor where they met Miss Gladys. Her mistress and sister put on their gloves, gathered their opera glasses, purses and evening wraps and exited the house to the waiting limousine.

Sally instructed Rose to clear the table, finish the dusting and lay out her mistress' bedclothes.

"When you are done, you may put on your page's uniform and rest in the parlor until the ladies return about midnight. You may take off your shoes and rest on the couch opposite your lady's and sleep. You will admit the ladies when they return. This is your evening of quiet and I leave you alone to your tasks."

Rose ascended to her room and dressed in her pretty boy clothes, retaining her high-heeled slippers and silken gloves. Let it not enter his mind for a moment that he was ever free from service.

He selected a book from the library in his room and repaired to the parlor, where he read for about an hour. Then he put down his book and contemplated his efforts to learn about the feminine world and about his own love of submission. How would he reconcile this private world with the world outside?

He looked up to the magnificent painting on the wall above the couch, a very large canvas in the Romantic style, showing a young

Rose Alone

French peasant girl in a garden. She is alone in front of her small cabin but she looks up as if listening. It is Joan of Arc, listening to the voices of angels which command her to service. Rose thinks of how beautiful the girl is. How frightening must be the task before her, for she must transform herself into something she is not – a warrior – in order to serve her master, the Lord God. She will suffer greatly in the metamorphosis itself, and she will also suffer at the hands of those who do not understand how a woman can make herself a man.

Inspired by the passion of the painting, Rose gathered together some paper and pens from the library began to draw a picture. It was a picture of himself as a beautiful page boy kneeling at the feet of his Goddess.

After this, Rose felt tired. He removed this shoes, stretched his silken legs and gave himself to sleep.

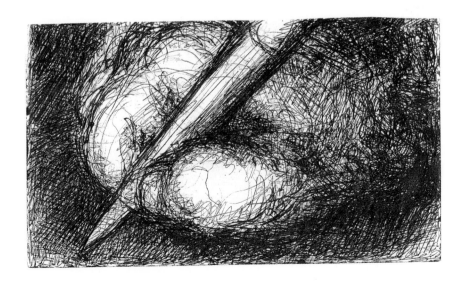

THE SCHOOL
FOR PAGES

t was the next morning and Lady Gladys announced that she was leaving town for a week to visit a friend. She informed Mary that during this period she would take over the responsibilities of the household and that Rose would be placed in a School for Pages, where he would receive more training in the arts appropriate to a servant.

"Rose, dear, you will prepare a small travelling bag with towels, night gown, toilet articles and extra hose and body suit. You will wear your page costume under your man's clothes. Sally will help you."

"I understand, my lady," said Rose, "and shall do my best to learn as always."

Rose prepared in mind and in dress for this important change of plans and was ready at the door when his lady arrived for imminent departure. Sally had her travelling bag and Rose his small bag.

When the limousine arrived, they all descended the stairs to the street and Mary embraced Rose in fond farewell.

Rose sat beside his lady and observed the passing scene as the vehicle moved up the West Side Highway and out of the city and finally into the countryside of Connecticut. In two hours time, they entered a formal estate surrounded by a high iron fence. There were formal gardens and hedges and a long alley of trees. Then they entered a courtyard and were received at the entrance by a splendid butler and led into a Renaissance Palace.

The butler presented the guests to a Lady secretary who led them to a reception room where Lady Gladys was graciously received and seated. It seemed that all arrangements had been made for Rose, who

The School for Pages

was put into the charge of a lady officer and led away, after being allowed to kiss his lady and promise to be good.

The formidable officer addressed Rose perfunctorily. "You may address me as Mother Jones." Rose observed that his guide wore a kind of uniform, like a nurse but with a soldierly air, and that she seemed to be an officer because of the deference paid her be similarly dressed persons whom they passed on the way.

Rose was taken to a large chamber, a dormitory with two rows of beds, where he was awaited by a page in colorful livery, who was introduced as Jane.

"Rose, I leave you in Jane's care. You will show him every attention and obedience, for he is your senior in this school. Do you understand?"

"Mother Jones, I thank you. I shall be good."

And the stately officer left Rose and Miss Jane to their duties.

Jane commanded Rose to undress and put his manly clothing in the chest at the foot of his bed. He resumed his page's uniform, the wig, the gloves and the slippers.

When he was ready and inspected, Miss Jane informed him of the rules of the school.

"All of the supervisors and governesses of this school are true women and lesbians. They regard us as tender children, girls - males who would be girls and yet cannot be, so we are bound to perpetual childhood. We must always defer to the women who lead us, for this is a perfect matriarchy and we are the servants who serve the women in every way.

"No communication is allowed between fellow pages in the school - only choral harmony in singing. We are supervised night and day and at meals. All living is in female attire and all movement is in pairs, as you will soon see. The female dress includes a face veil which precludes communication. In training or on station duties the boys wear page's uniforms. These are in the livery color of the boys' mistresses.

"Some boys have not yet been adopted. They wear the livery of the school until such time as they are chosen by a master or mistress, when they will wear the colors of their owner.

"Your training includes service outside of the school, whether in choral performances or as servants for hire. You are thus allowed to show your happiness in your state of bondage and to give yourself wholeheartedly to the service of whomever you are assigned to. Movements outside of the school are within a dark vehicle, but you will learn more of that this weekend.

"You will now learn some of the arts which you must use to entertain and delight your mistress. Do you understand? This is the last time we will speak."

Rose nodded his assent.

Princes in the Tower

Jane then provided him with a lovely small booklet which he was to keep with him always, entitled: *Credo of the Household Page.*

Jane then led him to the great mirrored dancing room where other pages were doing their footsteps and stretches at the bar. There he was delivered to the dance instructor, an efficient and commanding woman, who instructed him as follows:

"Rose, my dear, as you can observe, here we learn to dance. In a seminary they make priests and are taught to pray. In a military school they make soldiers who are taught to drill. Here in this school for pages we make graceful servants who dance and sing in beautiful harmony. So you, my boy, shall learn to dance beautifully."

Rose was taken in charge and led to a dressing room where he was fitted with ballet slippers. He was taught how to bind his feet tightly with pink ribbons into the shoes and how to stand on his toes like a ballerina. Rose was only able to walk on his toes for a few moments at a time but essayed some steps and vowed to himself to become grace-ful for his mistress.

On the first day he was trained in a some simple movements.

"At my command you will put your right foot forward. Such a pret-ty foot! You will respond to the tap of my baton. Now!"

Rose loved the movements, especially the slower ones, but he would need practice and conditioning before he was adept at the quick steps.

Rose rests from his dancing to contemplate his present role in the School for Pages. Being observed thus unoccupied, he is approached by a trainer and confiscated for duty. He is led away to a room con-taining many forms of equipment for training or restricting the move-ment of pages. Another page stands in the room awaiting assignment.

Without speaking a word, the trainer removes a pine board from a table. The board has a stiff harness attached to either end. Rose watch-es as the other page is strapped to the board, which is placed between his legs and raised to his crotch. The denim harness is then passed over his shoulders and secured at the waist by a belt of the same mate-rial.

Now Rose is roughly turned so that his back faces the other page. He stands about three paces in front, the page behind facing him. Then the board is brought up between Rose's legs and he is similarly secured to the denim and bodice. The board presses hard against his scrotum.

"Now walk!" is the command. No further instructions are needed. Rose finds that he must move in harmony with the page boy behind. Not a word is spoken. Thus are the boys left to themselves to learn coordination. They are captured together.

Without further instruction the boys are left to themselves to find a common activity. They walk around the empty room, then attempt some side steps and some kicks, then some rhythmic dance. The boy behind is perforce passive, following Rose's lead. They cannot communicate for they are muzzled.

At last Rose undertakes to convey to his partner that they should attempt to rest. Carefully Rose descends to his right knee, then backwards to his right buttocks. He rest his weight on his hand, then his elbow, toppling by degrees until his head rests on his gloved hands. The boys rest on the cold floor, making wriggling movements to keep warm.

They are to learn that this bondage together is to continue throughout the period of their schooling. If called to meals, they kneel and eat from the trays on the floor. The pole between them forces them to learn to move in absolute harmony, and if there is any purpose in all this, it is to impress upon these youths their total dependence. They are there to entertain their many mistresses who enjoy watching the boys manage their confinement with grace.

The School for Pages emphasizes sex, for the pages are essentially being groomed to be sexual objects. All the lines of their bodice focus on the penis, which is prominently supported by a codpiece over the stockings. The boys carry their penises as a sign of manhood, contrasting sharply with their delicacy of clothing and manners, their hairstyle, gloves, slippers and veil.

When a page reports to an officer for duty, he genuflects and displays his penis erectus, as he would his most vital and vulnerable organs. Thus he is at the mercy of whosoever controls him at the moment. Like a courtesan, the page offers himself as directed, appealing to the master in man, to the mistress in woman, to be gentle and merciful in their use of him.

See how prettily he dances for your pleasure, sings for your pleasure, serves for your aggrandizement. He is your foil - his submission will make you grow in power and stature and wisdom.

CREDO OF THE HOUSEHOLD PAGE

Q. What are my feet for?
A. To trip lightly and daintily on tiptoe to the bidding of my mistress.

Q. What are my ankles for?
A. To symbolize the idea of enchainment. They are held together neatly when standing.

Q. What are my knees for?
A. To be the symbol of my devotion and worship of my mistress. They are always slightly bent in her presence.

Q. What are my thighs, groin and body for?
A. To form a tightly bound foundation for support of clinging dress.

Q. What are my arms for?
A. To display pretty lingerie. The elbows are kept in towards the body.

Q. What are my wrists for?
A. To symbolize bondage of the arms. Bracelets and glove buttons suggest that symbol.

Q. What are my hands for?
A. For only the most precious holding. Always gloved.

Q. What are my neck and shoulders for?
A. For ready submission and punishment. Decolleté exposes the throat at all times for this purpose.

Q. What are my head and face for?
A. To be lovely but featureless. The wig and face net disguise masculine coarseness.

In sum: I am a lovely appendage and somewhat useful ornament in my lady's household.

The next weekend there is a great event, and all of the students in the school are connected together by a chain through a special loop at the crotch. They are put in darkened vehicles and taken to a great hall nearby. There is great excitement, for patrons will be coming from all over the country to view the pages in performance and make their selections.

Except for Rose and the other novices who must wait on tables, all of the pages are led in a parade, circling around the tables of the patrons and then up to the stage where they do a marvellous choral dance, all lined up on a chain passing from scrotum to scrotum and between the legs. They all stand for applause.

It is the finale of the evening, and a few students who have been deemed suitable for outside service will be sold as slaves to the highest bidders in the audience. Some of the engagements will indeed be difficult for the boys to bear and maintain a submissive composure, especially in single sex engagements.

Those who are not purchased will return to the school, where they are made to lie on a rug, still back to front, with one glass of water and a bottle which they use as a urinal. Each is covered with a sheet, the lights are extinguished and they are lulled to sleep with soothing music from a recorder.

At the sound of a drum roll, Mother Jones appears on the stage with a large man. He struggles against her, but cannot break free

The School for Pages

because his muzzle will suffocate him if he does not follow her every move. This rugged man sulks under his enforced restraint. He is a prisoner condemned to slavery. His captor is amused to reduce this dangerous man into a docile servant as one would break and domesticate a wild horse. He is wild and brutish and in the process of being brought under control. His aspirations will be turned to service and love for his master. His reward will be his own refinement and beauty, in wearing his master's livery. The pages and audience are in awe of this vision of manhood curbed.

Rose watches the slave auction with both horror and relief, grateful that he has already been adopted by his goddess. He does not want to serve anyone but his Mistress Gladys. Rose is holding a tray of beer mugs and a pitcher of beer, which he is bound to deliver to the patrons.

When in service, it is natural for patrons to feel the thighs and scrotum of the serving boys, who sense the compliment and pause

until released. "Master!" he must say in ecstatic acknowledgement as a crude patron seizes his scrotum and holds it in his fist. A large man, loudly complimenting Rose's delicate form, grabs him as he passes by with the laden tray. Then the patron steps on the boy's foot and gives pain as well as affirming ownership. The crude man is soliciting Rose for private service. Mother Jones takes note and will bill his account for Rose's work.

Rose is in a panic - must he go with this man? Must he show his willingness to serve by serving someone other than his mistress? This is terrible. Oh, would that his mistress Gladys come rescue him from this frightening prospect!

"Rose! Rose, my dear, wake up. You have been napping and we have returned from the opera."

It is the beautiful voice of his Goddess. It was all just a dream, a horrible, delicious nightmare.

Slave Market

LADY'S MAID

ose awoke early, but did not disturb his lady until she stirred. He lay quietly thinking of the course of events. He was glad that the school for pages was just a dream but was confused by his own excitement at the memory.

Miss Gladys awoke and kissed Rose passionately.

"Come, my darling. You and I shall bathe together this morning. So undress quickly and you and I shall put on bathing caps. Remember that your natural hair is to grow from now on."

They undressed and went into the shower together, as if they were man and wife. Rose was transported by this new familiarity and intimacy. What new things was he to learn now?

"Ah, my what a lovely youthful figure you have," she said as she admired his nakedness. He in turn loved her beauty, which was that of a goddess. They washed each other with soapy washcloths and rinsed. Gladys felt him all over and enjoyed the firm feel of his washed penis which she claimed as hers alone. Emerging from a cold rinse, they dried each other. Together they embraced and Rose felt his penis rise in excitement.

"Oh, my little man, it is too early for sex between us. "

Rose controlled his manly impulses as they dressed.

"After you serve us breakfast, I will give you a lesson in dressing me."

"Yes, my lady."

After a breakfast of toast and jam, Rose returned to Miss Gladys' room. He knocked and was admitted. He found his lady combing and brushing her hair.

" Now you will learn to put on my stockings and secure them to my corset."

Rose knelt to do this, inserting his hand deep into each stocking and bringing the fabric to a bunch; then delicately drawing it over the toes and heel and up the leg.

Gladys put a hand on Rose's back as he secured the clamps.

"Now, get my black shoes with the bow and fit them on."

Oh, such lovely feet and ankles, thought Rose. And the feel of those transparent gossamer stockings! This is womanhood!

Lady's Maid

"Now, remove my robe and bring me my red cloth dress. Later you shall learn how to do my undergarments."

Rose fetched the shimmering garment, fairly shimmering himself with love and gratitude.

"Gather the dress so that you can bring it over my head and shoulders. Good. Now draw down the skirt and secure the waist. Be very careful not to disarrange my hair."

This was how Rose spent the entire summer, learning the mysteries of the feminine world and growing stronger in his sense of self.

In the Fall Gerald went to Harvard and studied art, always wearing the straps beneath his clothes which bound him to his lady mistress. Every school break he would visit Mary and Gladys in New York and resume his training as a lady's maid. At other times Mary and Gladys were travelling, Mary gaining health and strength and character to the point that the next spring she was married to a splendid and handsome Italian artist. Mary and Gerald's parents finally came to recognize the independent spirit of their daughter and acknowledge her happiness.

Gerald also gained recognition at his school for his artwork, which was filled a with beauty and passion that he had developed in his service to the Lady Gladys.

Thus it was that early the following year his goddess spoke to him: "Now, my dear, you have served me well and you are ready to receive my gratitude. You have truly grown into a man in the true sense of manhood, for you have found your own inner purpose and your own soul. I have a surprise for you. It is now my chance to symbolically bind myself to you as you have bound yourself to me."

Rose knelt at his mistress' feet in ecstasy.

MARRIAGE

he Great Lady assembled Mary and Sally and Rose together in the great dining room and announced that this day there would be a private symbolic marriage of herself and Rose. She assigned to Sally the task of preparing Rose with veil and headband. Thus clothed, Rose was to remain in seclusion for two hours and meditate upon the great step that he would be taking in becoming her husband for life. The ceremony was scheduled for 4 o'clock. There was a solemnity to this occasion that held all in a silent spell.

Rose was taken in charge by Sally and led up the stairs to his robing room. He was instructed to undress and bathe as before. Then he was clothed in a long white silk dress and gloves and veiled and perfumed with lilac. Thus robed and holding a little cameo locket, a portrait of his lady, he was led to the great mirror and allowed to kneel before his own image in an attitude of prayer. A great lace veil was draped over his head and laid about his kneeling figure like a cascade of water.

He was left to contemplate of his great role of husband-in-waiting. The door clicked shut and the key turned in the lock.

Like a knight preparing for knighthood or a nun preparing for consecration, Rose gave himself to thoughts of his joyous servitude and its meaning for his future.

Let us assume that everyone has a secret force inside him. It is a very tender thing he has, which he keeps private. He doesn't understand it - it can either sublimate and become glorious or it can become hideous. If he can find an expression for his soul, clothe it, give it a role

with passion and excitement, this can become a catalyst and a way of awakening joy in life.

We all have a tender soul, a doppelganger. This tender soul attends us wherever we are. It is like a genii that lives within us, able to almost magically grant wishes, as soon as we understand what those wishes are. If treated well it gains in beauty and brilliance. It is a servant and a picture of beauty which is an image of grace. It is the ideal feminine and it is a muse for artistic expression. For Gerald this secret force, this tender servant, is Rose.

So in the purity of his white vesture and veiled in his inner life, Gerald Rose gives himself to dedication and devotion, contemplating his goddess' image. He feels the full extension of his penis under the robes and knows that his psyche is responding in full to the solemnity of this ritual.

Gerald now understands his own nature. Gerald Rose is ready to triumph in the art of life.

After nearly fainting from his long kneeling, Gerald Rose was recalled to life by Sally who took his hands and caused him to rise, carefully holding the skirts free as he stepped and kicked. Not a word was said. Leading him to the stairs, Sally instructed him to hold his skirts with his left hand and the stair rail with his right as he descended the carpeted stairs. She held his elbow all the way.

Led as a votive offering, he was taken to his lady and caused to kneel.

His lady lifted the great veil and circled his neck with a white collar of silk and a pearl necklace, then kissed him through his face veil.

Then she pronounced the words of his vows, which he repeated after her.

"I, Gerald Graham, surnamed Rose, do hereby submit myself, body, soul, and spirit, to the will and pleasure of my great mistress Gladys, to serve her all the days of her life. In token of this pledge, I herewith place my hands in hers in total submission."

When Rose had finished his vow of marriage and kissed the hands and feet of his lady, he was instructed to rise and stand in the presence of his lady, Sally and his sister Mary. All present embraced him and loved him.

Then the Lady Gladys bound her husband's wrists with a silken band and guided him to the dining room where Sally seated her lady. The husband knelt on a footstool at his Lady's side. Sally then served a symbolic meal of pudding to the lady, who fed her husband and herself.

The lady restored her husband's veil and then, in the presence of Mary and Sally, addressed her new husband as follows, holding his head close to her side.

"Now, my dear, you have completed your training in noble manhood and are worthy to be my husband whom I love. Although in our private life you will remain my faithful lady's maid Rose and occasionally receive the punishments due a page boy, you have now entered the world of manhood and are truly my husband. You, Gerald Rose, will grow in stature and be worthy of reverence in this house and among men. Your pledge to me will be your strength and source of wisdom. And the art which you shall pursue with passion shall be your claim to manhood. Now you are a man because you have your mistress and your vocation. Together we shall do great things in the world."

"Rise now and greet your sister Mary, your nurse Sally and myself."

"Now let us all to bed."

END

Marriage

POSTLUDE

he solution here experienced by Gerald and Mary to their problem of meeting adulthood is individual and not to be taken as universally applicable. It is a magical solution to my own childhood difficulties and those of my poor sister.

My sister, Mary Henderson McKesson, was six years my senior. She was a loving person. She attended Spence School where she was loved by her classmates. She had a grand debut at The Ritz Carlton, which I attended after the dinner, being under age. As a child, she wanted to celebrate my birthday with little secret gifts, many referring to Winken Blinken and Nod, from our favorite book. She read the book before I could do so. Mary was isolated from her brothers and had no sister; perhaps I was a disappointment to her, being no sister. She traveled to Europe with us and responded to Italian life and art. I sang in a chorus with her at a Mexican Cultural Festival. She attended Badminton Club, but only to socialize, not to play. She became overweight and unhappy and was continually abused by my mother for untruthfulness. She found no love. She suffered because of the death of my oldest brother, Jack, killed in a motorcycle accident on the way to Harvard in his freshman year. She accused me of cruelty in supporting my mother in her accusations against her. She died in 1936. I was not told the cause of death but assumed depression. I'm sure I was not a loving brother though I shared with her the care of her macaw Alibaba. Mary is supposed to have had two love affairs, one with an impecunious Spanish nobleman and another when she was taken from an elopement by my mother and whisked off to a

Pedagogue

Caribbean cruise where she acquired the parrot in Cartagena. The man was a Dutchman named Bloom, an engineer, I believe. My mother made up an elaborate memory book for Mary. This is lost. Mama assumed all Mary's friendships in her conscious souvenirs. Mary was an appendage of her mother.

I too had an unhappy youth at boarding school and was a poor student. I began my experiments in transvestism in my sophomore year of college. I thus developed a secret life which strengthened me in my search for a profession and a future.

The mythical Gladys materializes in real life as Madeline Mason, true wife of Malcolm (the author), she a true poet, and he an artist.

Every young adult has need of a guide to young adulthood in affluent society so that the challenges of life may be met with fortitude derived from a sense of worth, and acceptance of responsibilities for his or her private destiny.

Let it be added that life in the body is indeed a condition of bondage and can benefit by acceptance of this condition.

Malcolm McKesson
6.1.96

Postlude

Two Servants Kiss

M

M

A SELECTION
OF DRAWINGS
WITH TEXT

III

Three school children in a subway train on an excursion.
All are dressed alike, but one is a boy 15 years old.

I am ten years old. See my pretty frock.
It is my birthday present.

Girlhood.
Lace dress for boys, very dainty.
Skipping rope for the amusement of his mistress.

Croquet - Recreation at the School for Pages.
Being a page is like being a monk - you have committed yourself to a lifetime in service and must never take off the costume which signifies your devotion.

Page boy livery - embroidered. Store window -
a woman's shop in London where women buy the vesture for pages.
"What darling little pigeon breasts! I must bring Jean with me to be fitted for
this style – Oh, my dear, must he look cute!"
"Just too sweet, darling!"

*Page boy delivered in a box. It was a heavy box shaped like a flower
delivery and bound with a broad pink ribbon.
Imagine the surprise and the delight to find this lovely boy.*

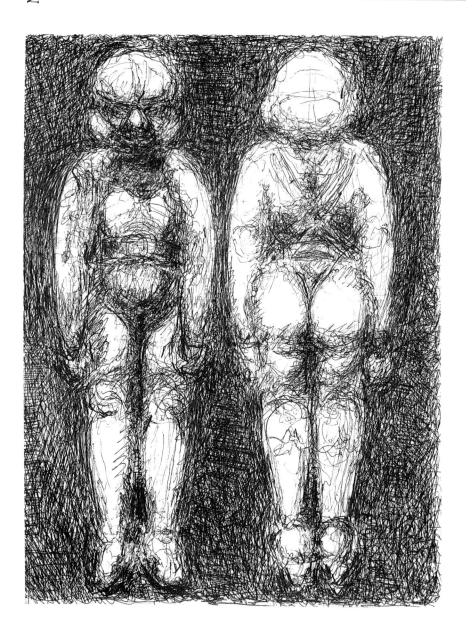

Two call-boys pass each other in the hallway, eye each other and pass on silently.

We are led into service. "Come along children."
Some are bound. Perhaps some of us have been spoken for.
We did not know what we had let ourselves in for.

This book is dedicated to Madeline Mason.

List of Illustrations

All illustrations collection of Henry Boxer Gallery unless otherwise noted.

Special thanks to Henry Boxer for spectacular support and assistance with gathering the materials for this book. Thanks also to John Phelan, for typing out the original manuscript and to Martin Wilner, MD for introducing us to Malcolm.

And last but not least to all of Malcolm's collectors, who generously allowed us to use the images in their collections: Daniel Raymond Anthony, Ray and Jodi Benson, Roger Cardinal, Eric and Patty Cole, Judy and Arthur Gold, James Hornbeak, Joan Pearlman, Steve and Beth Phillips, Monty Powell, Richard and Lois Rosenthal, Jeff Ross, Geff Rushton, Elyse Saperstein, Jack and Nanette Stevens, Angela Usry at North Shore Gallery, and Michael Zients.